THE HEART OF THE MATTER

After the award-winning screenwriter Dominic Talbot leaves his briefcase in the back of one of Georgia Jones's cabs, she ends up working as his personal on-set driver. Despite his apparent romantic entanglement with leading lady Belle Jeffreys, Georgia finds her heart warming towards him. However, trouble haunts the film set. Dominic scoffs at the notion of a curse — until a cameraman breaks a leg, a fire breaks out, and the leading man catches chicken-pox . . .

Books by Margaret Mounsdon
in the Linford Romance Library:

THE MIMOSA SUMMER
THE ITALIAN LAKE
LONG SHADOWS
FOLLOW YOUR HEART
AN ACT OF LOVE
HOLD ME CLOSE
A MATTER OF PRIDE
SONG OF MY HEART
MEMORIES OF LOVE
WRITTEN IN THE STARS
MY SECRET LOVE
A CHANCE ENCOUNTER
SECOND TIME AROUND

MARGARET MOUNSDON

THE HEART OF THE MATTER

Complete and Unabridged

LINFORD
Leicester

First published in Great Britain in 2012

First Linford Edition
published 2013

British Library CIP Data

Mounsdon, Margaret.
The heart of the matter. - -
(Linford romance library)
1. Love stories.
2. Large type books.
I. Title II. Series
823.9'2-dc23

ISBN 978-1-4448-1432-3

Published by
F. A. Thorpe (Publishing)
Anstey, Leicestershire

Set by Words & Graphics Ltd.
Anstey, Leicestershire
Printed and bound in Great Britain by
T. J. International Ltd., Padstow, Cornwall

This book is printed on acid-free paper

SPECIAL MESSAGE TO READERS

THE ULVERSCROFT FOUNDATION
(registered UK charity number 264873)
was established in 1972 to provide funds for research, diagnosis and treatment of eye diseases. Examples of major projects funded by the Ulverscroft Foundation are:-

- The Children's Eye Unit at Moorfields Eye Hospital, London
- The Ulverscroft Children's Eye Unit at Great Ormond Street Hospital for Sick Children
- Funding research into eye diseases and treatment at the Department of Ophthalmology, University of Leicester
- The Ulverscroft Vision Research Group, Institute of Child Health
- Twin operating theatres at the Western Ophthalmic Hospital, London
- The Chair of Ophthalmology at the Royal Australian College of Ophthalmologists

You can help further the work of the Foundation by making a donation or leaving a legacy. Every contribution is gratefully received. If you would like to help support the Foundation or require further information, please contact:

THE ULVERSCROFT FOUNDATION
The Green, Bradgate Road, Anstey
Leicester LE7 7FU, England
Tel: (0116) 236 4325

website: www.foundation.ulverscroft.com

'You Work Too Hard'

'Sorry, Georgia.' Jake's ears turned an even deeper shade of red than their usual healthy outdoor colour. He lowered his gaze to the floor unable to look Georgia in the eye. She stared at him in dismay. This was the third occasion in as many weeks that he'd done something wrong. She could almost hear the discontented mutterings of the other drivers.

'You'll have to fill in an incident report,' she said with a sigh.

'I know.'

'What happened this time?' she asked.

'I dropped the fare off at the station. We'd made the journey in record time. He was late for his, train you see.' Jake gulped and took another deep breath before continuing with his story. 'It was already in the station when we got there and looked about to leave so the fare threw some notes at me telling me to keep the change before dashing on to the platform. I dropped one of the notes in the foot well and was busy picking it up and I didn't notice he'd left his briefcase on the seat until after the train had gone.' Jake ground to a halt and waited for Georgia to react.

She stifled another sigh. This sort of thing did happen from time to time, but right now it could prove to be more than an embarrassing lapse of service. New Cabs, the company run by Abe Shand, Jake's father, was attempting to outbid them at every turn by undercutting their costs. They had already poached several of Georgia's valued customers and a new account had been snatched from under her nose only the day before.

'Their rates were more competitive,' had been the embarrassed explanation from the manager of an engineering firm when Georgia had telephoned to find out the reason why.

'I know this doesn't look good. Everyone will think I did it on purpose, won't they?'

‘A passenger’s property is his own responsibility,’ Georgia evaded a direct answer then taking pity on Jake’s discomfort added, ‘It wasn’t your fault.’

Although she would never admit it, a part of her couldn’t help wondering if he were being economical with the truth. Jake had denied it vehemently but it was possible he had overlooked the briefcase because his father had told him to. Abe Shand was a very dominant character and Georgia was sure he wouldn’t be above using his gentle-natured son to undermine Georgia Cabs’ integrity to New Cabs’ advantage.

Jake wasn’t one of Georgia’s regular drivers but being an old college companion of hers, he occasionally covered when they were under pressure. More than once he had stepped in at short notice and Georgia was reluctant to blame him for what might have been a simple mistake that anyone could have made.

Today when the driver scheduled for

the station run had called in sick and they'd had a last-minute request for a cab Jake had volunteered to take his place.

Jake pointed to the expensive-looking tooled leather tag. 'It's got a business card attached.'

'I'll give the number a ring.' Georgia glanced at it. It wasn't one she recognised and she hoped the fare hadn't been a new client.

'Not your lucky day, is it?' Jake nodded towards another briefcase that had been handed in earlier. 'Had a run on them, have you?'

'You know Saturday afternoons, always a busy time, especially if there's been a race meeting.'

The local racecourse was trying to build up business and Georgia, keen to encourage their custom, had arranged a special deal for their patrons.

'So are we still on for tonight?' Jake asked.

'Tonight?' Georgia fiddled with a paper clip as she tried to decipher a scrawled message taken by the afternoon operator.

'It's quiz night.'

Georgia stared blankly at Jake.

'At The Duck?' he prompted her.

Georgia had completely forgotten his invitation. She knew she was blushing as she said, 'Sorry to be a party pooper, Jake, but I ought to stay on.'

'You need a break some time, Georgia,' Jake insisted. 'Your parents didn't expect you to work twenty-four-seven during their absence.'

'I know.' She ran a hand through her hair. It badly needed a cut. Her shirt, too, was sticking to her back after a day sitting cramped in the tiny control centre, the hub of the family mini-cab company, 'Only the night cover man is new. I'm sure he's perfectly competent but I don't want any more mix-ups.'

Her parents were ten days into a six-month break in Australia, to visit Georgia's brother, his wife and new baby. Her father hadn't wanted to take such a long break but Georgia had insisted.

'I can run things in your absence and you know how Patsy hates being put in kennels,' she had said, referring to their miniature long-haired dachshund.

'Don't you want to see Nick?' her father had asked. 'You need a holiday as much as we do.'

'Of course I do,' Georgia had replied, 'but I can always visit him another time, perhaps during our winter when it's summer out there? I know the ropes here and you don't want New Cabs muscling in on the business in your absence, do you?'

'I suppose not,' her father agreed reluctantly.

'Besides, with modern technology we won't be out of touch with each other. I shall expect frequent video links of the new baby, your first grandchild, Mum,' she coaxed.

This had swayed her mother and eventually Georgia had convinced both her parents to take their holiday. So far everything had run smoothly, although it had placed a heavy responsibility on

Georgia's shoulders. She couldn't remember when she had last taken a day off. She enjoyed the work but her hours were long and arduous and there was little time for a social life.

'You work too hard,' Jake chided her.

'I need to,' Georgia insisted.

'Surely you can take one night off?'

'I'll join you later if I can,' Georgia said, her mind already on next week's schedules.

After he'd gone Georgia immersed herself in sorting out the drivers' rota. She nibbled on a cheese sandwich that had been on her desk since lunchtime and which she had only now got around to eating. The cheese tasted stale and the bread was curling at the edges but she was so hungry she didn't notice.

A lot of their business came from the local stud, affiliated to the racecourse and the manager had informed her that next week they were expecting some important visitors from Ireland. Georgia wanted to make sure there were enough drivers on the standby list should there be extra demand. With rumours of a flu bug sweeping through the village, she didn't want an epidemic decimating the workforce.

The local art centre, too, was running some specials. A weaving week was planned along with a painting retreat and the wildlife sanctuary was holding a special bird-watching weekend. Barn owls were nesting in some old ruins and a posting about it on the internet had created a flurry of interest.

The coming weeks were going to be more than busy, Georgia thought as she bit her lip. So far she had lost none of her drivers to New Cabs, but there was always the risk they could be tempted away on the promise of higher rates of pay. It was a cut-throat business and Georgia was determined to stay ahead of the game. She thrived on the challenge. It had given her a new purpose in life after the break-up of her engagement and she wouldn't have it any other way even if it meant she fell asleep every night the moment her head touched the pillow.

The village of Dod Stretton wasn't text book chocolate box, but it did possess a certain charm. An impressive Norman church dominated the Fenland village amid sleepy timbered cottages, unchanged from the days when the economy had thrived from wool and silk weaving. The local heritage museum displayed many fine examples of its past glory and the resurgence of interest in home crafts meant the area was once again featuring on the tourist map.

Georgia was glad when one of the conglomerates had lost interest in Dod Manor. To develop the 16th Century moated manor house into a leisure complex would, she felt, have robbed it of its charm, even though parts of it had been sorely neglected over the years.

Abe Shand didn't share her views on that one. He saw any possible development as a way to extend his business. Georgia supposed his views highlighted the difference between the two companies. Georgia wasn't against progress, but not at the expense of the environment.

Efforts had frequently been made to restore Dod Manor to its former glory, but the task had proved daunting for the incumbents and the house had been left unoccupied for several years after the last of the family moved out.

'Have you heard the latest?' One of the drivers poked his head through the door.

Georgia smiled up at him. 'Not another briefcase left on a back seat?'

'Better than that. There's a story doing the rounds that a costume drama is going to be filmed at Dod Manor.'

'Where did you get that one from?' Georgia asked.

'One of the regular taxi drivers at the station told me. Said he had some award-winning screenwriter in his taxi the other day.'

'They'll have their work cut out if they do use the Manor. Last I heard the roof leaked and there was severe dry rot in the timbers. That's why everyone's pulled out.'

'Parts of it aren't too bad. Anyway, thought you'd like to know the word on the street.'

'I'll believe it when I find a superstar sitting in the back of one of my cabs,' Georgia replied with a smile.

'If it's true do you think I could get a bit part as an extra?' The overweight driver twirled round. 'I can see myself strutting my stuff across the heath in breeches and a wet shirt, can't you?' He grinned at Georgia.

With a cheery wave, he clocked out, leaving Georgia to juggle with her figures. By the time she was through she realised it was nearly ten, far too late to join the others for the quiz evening.

'You are turning into a hermit,' she muttered under her breath.

'What was that?' the night cover called over. 'Did you say something?'

'Everything OK?' she called back.

'It's quiet,' he replied, 'but no problems.'

'You've got my mobile number if you need me.'

'Off home?' he asked.

'After I've made a couple of telephone calls,' Georgia replied as she dialled the number Jake had found on the briefcase.

'Hello,' she said, after the answering machine had finished relaying its message. 'Georgia Cabs calling regarding a briefcase found in one of our vehicles. Perhaps the owner would like to call this number.' She reeled it off.

What Georgia needed now was a good hot bath, perhaps a bowl of soup, then she intended to curl up and watch a film she had recorded days ago and still not got around to watching.

Waving goodbye Georgia strode out into the night air. At this time of year it didn't get dark until late and the sky was the bruised purple of twilight.

The control centre was situated in what had once been an old telephone exchange, adjacent to her parents' cottage and on the edge of a disused airfield. Georgia's brother used to tease her when they were children, telling her it was still haunted by the ghosts of past flyers. Many brave young men had flown their last missions from the base during the war and Georgia's parents always insisted she and her brother treated the landing strip with respect.

Georgia continued walking to the cottage. It seemed strange living back at home again. She had valued the independence of having her own flat, but with Max still occupying his apartment in the same block, she'd had no wish to bump into him and his new girlfriend in the lift or on the stairs, and so she had made the decision to return home.

Her father had suggested she occupy what had once been the granny flat he had built over their private garage for his mother who had occupied the rooms until her death several years ago and now they made a perfect base for Georgia.

Patsy raced to greet her as Georgia

opened the door.

'Have you missed me?' Georgia bent down to stroke the silky ears. A warm tongue licked her fingers.

'Go on, out you go.' She shooed her outside. 'Five minutes,' she called after the black dart as it sped out of the gate and into the grass, the bell on her collar tinkling as she foraged for goodies.

There were no messages for her on the family phone and Georgia heaved a sigh of relief. Lately there had been enough drama to last her a lifetime and, until her parents returned, her personal life was going to have to be placed on hold.

Heating up her soup she flicked through the post. One or two bills, which she would attend to, she placed to one side. There was the usual mixture of junk mail and advertising flyers. Pouring soup into her mug, she sipped it as she went through the rest of the post.

Her fingers hovered over a handwritten letter addressed to her. The bold blue ink lettering on the envelope was unmistakeable. Her soup churned in her stomach.

The letter was from Max.

A Difficult Client

'I'm not sure where it is, sir.' The man on night cover was in the middle of shrugging on his coat.

'I haven't time to wait while you get your act together,' the customer snapped at him. 'I have to get to an important breakfast meeting. All this is most inconvenient.'

'I'm very sorry, sir.'

'Why can't you take better care of your customers' belongings?'

'A customer's belongings are his own responsibility, sir.' Jake, who had called in on the off-chance of bumping into Georgia, had overheard the exchange and was quick to point out. 'There is a notice to this effect in the back of all the cabs.'

'Yes, well there would be, wouldn't there?' The man snapped back at him. 'Any excuse to wriggle out of things.'

'That's hardly fair, sir.'

'Do you know the whereabouts of my briefcase?' He glared at Jake. 'I can't stand around all day arguing the finer points of responsibility.'

'Is this it?' Another driver who had been lingering around the call centre hoping for a fare held up a standard-sized briefcase.

'Yes. Thank goodness someone around here seems to know what's going on.'

He put out a hand to take it from the driver's grasp.

'If you'll just sign for it, sir?' Jake butted in again, intercepting the exchange.

'I'm in a hurry.'

'If you don't sign for it, we can't return your property to you,' Jake replied calmly, 'Miss Jones is most insistent on that one.'

'Give it here. I'd like a word with your Miss Jones,' the man muttered as he scrawled his signature at the bottom of a sheet of paper, 'about the way her staff handle issues.'

'Any time, sir.' Jake's smile gave

nothing away. 'We're always willing to help and we welcome customer feedback. Here's our card in case you have need of our services in the future.'

'I very much doubt I will.' He ignored the card. 'New Cabs will get my custom from now on. At least they know how to conduct an efficient organisation.'

The door banged to behind him.

'Sorry.' The night operator made a face. 'I made a bit of a hash of that one, didn't I? Thanks for your help.'

'Think nothing of it,' Jake reassured him.

'Perhaps I should stay on and explain to Georgia? Ray can't come in today as he's got a family party. I was hoping Georgia would be here to take over by now.'

'I'll cover for you. It's time you got back to your wife and the baby.'

'If you're sure?'

'That's what bachelors are for, covering for the new fathers. Off you go.'

Jake waved him off the premises then, alone in the control centre, he filed the briefcase receipt before making a mug of coffee. Some customers were like that, he mused. Nothing you did was right for them, yet others were the exact opposite. He supposed it was the same with life, rather like his relationship with Georgia, such as it was. Even if his father hadn't encouraged his son's attentions towards Georgia, Jake would have still felt an attraction.

'Now that brother of hers has moved to Australia I suspect her parents may want to follow his example. That would leave Georgia running the show. It would do our businesses no harm,' Abe had pointed out to Jake, 'if there were to be a family connection between us.'

'Georgia's still getting over Max Doyle,' Jake replied.

'Then give her a shoulder to cry on,' had been Abe's crisp reply.

The switchboard lit up and Jake turned his attention to the incoming call. No sooner had he finished booking a cab for a client than another call came through. It proved to be a busy morning, made busier by the rumour regarding the proposed filming at Dod Manor which Jake was beginning to suspect might be true. He frowned.

It was unlike Georgia not to come in on a Sunday, but if she had decided to take the day off, Jake did not want to disturb her. It was half-past four in the afternoon before Georgia finally put in an appearance.

'Jake. Hi.' Her voice sounded breathless as she rushed in. 'Anything happening?'

He glanced up and smiled. 'No need to look so worried,' he assured her. 'Everything's in hand.'

'Sorry,' she apologised. 'So no problems?'

'Not really. I've been fielding phone calls from the press about this supposed filming of a costume drama at Dod Manor.'

'Then it really is true?'

'It's a possibility. Someone seems to have got hold of the story and is spreading it about.'

Georgia cleared her throat. 'I'm sorry about last night, Jake, not getting to The Duck,' she said. 'Time ran away with me.'

'We won,' Jake replied, 'so we are through to the next round despite the loss of your encyclopaedic knowledge of art.'

Georgia broke into a smile. 'Well done. I'll keep my fingers crossed for you. Anything else to tell me?'

'Nearly forgot,' Jake retrieved the brief-case receipt from the file. 'The man who came to collect this was a bit rude. We may get some negative feedback.'

'What happened?'

'We couldn't find it. Then he was difficult about signing for it and I said I wouldn't pass it over until he did. He said he was too busy to fiddle around with forms. Usual stuff. I offered him one of our cards and said we were always pleased to hear from our customers.'

'Did it work?'

'Don't think so. He refused to take

the card and said New Cabs would get all his future business. Sorry.'

'Don't give it a second thought,' Georgia said, doing her best not to frown. Yet again Jake had managed to discredit them in favour of his father's business.

'How long have you been on duty?' Georgia asked, wondering how she could diplomatically suggest Jake should take a break.

'Ever since the night cover clocked off.'

'Why don't you get on home?' Georgia suggested.

'Well, I may just be in time to catch the football.'

'Go on then.'

She heard Jake power up his motorbike, mount the saddle and roar out of the business park complex leaving a strong smell of exhaust fumes in his wake.

Georgia sat down at the switchboard and, after a quick familiarisation of the current bookings, extracted Max's letter from her bag.

Things hadn't worked out between

him and Kelly, Georgia read as she tucked a stray strand of hair behind her ear. Six months ago she would have been on the telephone like a shot, not caring about her loss of pride or the fact that he had gone off with one of her best friends, but as time passed and she had begun to get her life back together she knew she couldn't go through all the heartache again.

In classic tradition she had not known about Max's affair with Kelly until she received a text from another friend. The blow had come out of the blue and had been totally unexpected, even if it did explain the frequent absences and missed social occasions due to pressure of work.

A shadow was cast across her letter and she looked up to find a tall, impatient-looking man standing in front of her.

'When you've finished reading your personal correspondence,' he clipped at her, 'may I have a moment of your attention?'

Annoyed by the tone of his voice, Georgia carefully refolded Max's letter and put it back in her bag before smiling up at him.

'What can I do to help you, sir?' she asked.

She wished he wasn't quite so good looking although a scar in the middle of his forehead marred his physical appearance.

'Dominic Talbot,' he said and waited as if he expected Georgia to recognise his name.

'Yes?' she queried, hoping they hadn't forgotten to pick him up. 'Did you order a taxi?'

'I did.'

'When?'

'Yesterday.'

'What?' Georgia raised her voice in confusion. 'You haven't been waiting twenty-four hours?'

The suggestion of a smile softened his tanned face. 'No, your driver got me to the station on time but I forgot my briefcase in the back of the cab.

Someone left a message for me.'

'That was me,' Georgia replied. 'It's here.' Georgia looked round, then frowned. She searched the surrounding area. 'I'm sorry,' she apologised a few moments later. 'It doesn't seem to be where I left it.'

'What?' the man looked up from checking his mobile.

'Your briefcase. I put it in the cupboard.'

'Isn't it kept locked?'

'Well, no,' Georgia admitted.

'Why not? Don't you have a safe for valuables?'

'Yes, we do, but it's not very big so I put customers' misplaced belongings in the cupboard. It makes for easy access.'

'Too easy it would seem.' Dominic's voice sounded dangerously close to angry.

'It's a simple mix-up, nothing more, I'm sure.'

Georgia looked down at the signed receipt Jake had left on the table in front of her and began to suspect what had happened.

'I think it's been given to another customer in error,' she admitted in a tight voice.

'I don't believe it.' Dominic was no longer pretending to be polite. 'I thought Georgia Cabs was a professional organisation.'

'We had two briefcases left behind yesterday and I think they might have got confused.'

'It wasn't the bags that were confused. What sort of outfit are you running here?' he demanded. 'Who's the boss of this set up?'

'I am.' Georgia threw back her head and met the challenge in his eyes.

'You'd better get my briefcase back because if you don't there'll be trouble.'

'There is a disclaimer printed in the back of all our cabs,' Georgia pointed out, her voice wavering at the expression on the customer's face.

'I don't care if you've a whole charter of disclaimers, I want my briefcase and if I don't get it within the next twenty-four hours there'll be trouble.'

'I'll do my best, sir.' Georgia picked up a pen and hoped her hand wasn't shaking too much. 'If you could just refresh my memory regarding your details.'

'Here.' He flipped a business card on to the desk. 'You can get me on any of those numbers.'

Georgia blinked. One of her contact lenses had slipped, blurring the print on the card. If Dominic Talbot hadn't been looking at her so intently she would have wiped her eyes but she didn't want him to think she was being emotional or that she was upset by the encounter.

'I expect to hear from you soon. Hadn't you better get looking instead of just standing there?' He delivered his parting shot as he closed the office door firmly behind him.

Containing the urge to poke her tongue out at his retreating back, Georgia rubbed her sore eyes and adjusted her lens before taking a good look at the card.

'You know who that was?'

She jumped at the sound of an excited voice behind her.

'Terry?' It was one of her regular drivers.

'Hi.' He beamed at her. 'I came by to tell you about the man who collected a briefcase this morning.'

'Jake filled me in on the details,' Georgia replied. 'It seems we're not doing very well. We've given the wrong briefcase to the wrong man.'

'How can you be so sure? The man who's just been in here is Dominic Talbot.'

'I know he's given me his card.' Georgia looked at it again. 'It says here he's a screenwriter.'

'He is not only a screenwriter, he is an award-winning one and that's why I know we didn't give his briefcase to the other customer. I've seen Dominic Talbot on television lots of times.'

'But you haven't seen his briefcase.'

'That's where you're wrong.'

'Terry, what are you talking about?'

'I saw him interviewed on late night

television and he was telling the audience how he couldn't count the number of times his luggage had been lost on long-haul flights. It got so bad that he now hates to be separated from his bags so in order to easily identify them he always puts a bright red strap round the middle. The case I gave out to the other man didn't have a strap of any colour round it.'

'Then where is it?' Georgia demanded.

'We had a stationery delivery on Friday. It was still all over the floor this morning so Jake and I tidied it up.'

'You know drivers aren't supposed to interfere with the supplies.' Georgia knew she was sounding ungrateful but all the stress was shredding her nerves.

'We were only trying to help, what with your parents being away. You've been going through a tough time and we all want to do our bit,' Terry admitted, a crestfallen look on his face. 'We didn't want anyone tripping over files or anything.'

'Sorry, Terry,' Georgia apologised. 'It

was a sensible thing to do and I appreciate your thoughtfulness.' She crouched down on the floor beside him. 'What's that?' she asked, catching a glimpse of colour under the filing cabinet.

'It's here.' Terry tugged and with a cry of triumph pulled out a briefcase. 'See, bright red strap?'

'You are one brilliant boy.' Georgia grabbed out at it. 'I am not letting go of it until it's safely back in Mr Talbot's hands.'

She frowned as she clutched the case to her chest.

'Now what's wrong?' Terry demanded.

'He's going to think we are doubly inefficient when he finds out the briefcase was in the office all along. Hardly gives a professional image, does it?'

'It's up to you to use your charm to convince him we're not a hick outfit then, isn't it?'

Georgia bit her lip. Dominic Talbot looked as though he could very easily withstand her charm.

'I'll give it my best shot,' she promised.

Georgia suspected Dominic Talbot was not the sort of man who suffered fools gladly and that she would have her work cut out to convince him otherwise.

'You realise what this means, don't you?' Terry's eager smile was back on his face now they'd found the missing briefcase.

'No?'

'If Dominic Talbot has been commissioned to do the screenplay for this new costume drama that everyone's going on about then things must be at an advanced stage and we could be in business. I can see it now, cab drivers to the stars.'

'Before you get carried away,' Georgia cautioned him, 'we don't know anything of the sort so don't start spreading more rumours.'

'Why else would a writer of his stature be here?'

'Terry.' Georgia began to fear his enthusiasm was running away with him. 'I don't want you repeating any of this.

At the moment we know absolutely nothing about anything and we don't want to be accused of making wild accusations. We're already in enough trouble with Dominic Talbot as it is.'

'Spoilsport.' Terry grinned not in the least bit quelled by Georgia's put down. 'All right. I promise. When are you going to call him?'

Georgia picked up Dominic's business card. 'I'll do it from Dod Cottage. It's more private there. You never know who's listening in on the airwaves. I don't want New Cabs finding out about this. Will you stay and man the switchboard for me?'

'Sure. If Dominic is looking for a male lead, I'm available,' he added with a grin.

Georgia raised her eyebrows.

She picked up the briefcase and made her way down the stairs.

A Secret Meeting

'Come on, Patsy,' Georgia called through the kitchen door. 'Time for a walk.'

A dark shape of silky fur shot past her and out into the small garden in front of the cottage. Georgia ran after the dog and clipped on her lead.

'No you don't,' she admonished her. 'I've got a briefcase to deliver first.'

Georgia glanced at the telephone numbers Dominic had given her and realised with a start of pleasure that he was staying at The Duck.

Better and better, Georgia thought as Patsy settled down on the back seat of the cab. *No need to call him first and I can be in and out in ten minutes.*

The Duck car park was full and Georgia was forced to leave her car on the verge outside.

'You'd better come in with me, Patsy.' Georgia locked the driver's door.

Patsy did a few excited circles of the grass verge before trotting obediently beside Georgia as they made their way to The Duck.

'What's going on? Why's everyone double parked?' she called across to one of the kitchen staff sitting outside enjoying the late afternoon sunshine.

'Journalists,' he called back. 'They've got scent of a story. They're clogging up the bar.'

'What's it all about?'

'It seems Dod Manor is in the news. Someone's leaked a story about a film crew descending on us to suss out the location. First I've heard of it. Have you got wind of anything on the grapevine?'

'Only a bit of third-hand gossip, but you know how stories get exaggerated.'

'Tell me about it.'

'If the rumours are true,' Georgia said, 'I foresee problems.'

'You mean media vehicles clogging up the lanes?'

'Not to mention the preservation society.'

'Still it would be exciting, wouldn't it?'

'That's one way of putting it,' Georgia replied. 'Would you look after Patsy for me, Den?' she asked.

Georgia struggled to the main desk and tried to make her voice heard above the clamour all around her. She didn't recognise the receptionist on duty. Neither did she like to bellow out Dominic Talbot's name in case she blew his cover.

'Excuse me.' She beckoned to a harassed member of reception staff. 'Dominic Talbot,' she lowered her voice.

'He's not staying here,' she clipped back at Georgia before she had a chance to explain.

'I'm not a journalist.'

'I don't care who you are. Mr Talbot is not here.'

'I happen to know he is. You don't know if he's in his room, do you?'

'Nice try,' one of the journalists sidled up to Georgia, 'but it won't wash with that one. She's as frosty as a winter's day. I can't get a thing out of her. Don't know you, do I? Which agency are you with?'

'I'm not.'

'Freelance? Well, good luck. Let me know if you get a sniff of a lead.'

Sensing she was of no more use to him, the red-faced man sauntered away.

'Look,' Georgia gave it another try with the receptionist, 'I really do need to speak to Dominic Talbot as a matter of urgency.'

'And how many more times do I really need to tell you he isn't here?'

'Don't you recognise me?' Georgia asked in desperation. 'I'm part of Jake Shand's quiz team.'

'Well you weren't here last night, were you?'

'No,' Georgia conceded. 'I was working.'

Gritting her teeth in frustration Georgia turned over Dominic's business card. On the back was scrawled a room number.

She glanced quickly around the foyer. No-one was looking in her direction and she knew the way upstairs. Not giving herself time to think twice in case her courage failed her, she slipped through the dividing door that led to the rooms. Holding her breath and not hearing any outraged voice demanding to know what she was doing, Georgia headed for the stairs.

As with all old buildings the floor-boards creaked when she tried to tiptoe along the corridor. She hoped the noise in the bar downstairs would muffle her progress.

Georgia stopped by the door of what she hoped was Dominic's room and not a random number he had scrawled on the back of his card. The briefcase handle was digging into the flesh of her hand and the famous red strap was coming adrift but there wasn't time to fasten it now.

Straightening her shoulders Georgia gave a timid knock and waited. For a few moments nothing happened. Then to her horror she heard footsteps mounting the stairs. Any moment now her presence would be discovered. She raised her hand to knock on the door again, but before she could do so it was yanked open and it was only with the greatest difficulty that she was able to stop herself from hitting Dominic Talbot full in the face.

'What are you doing here?' he demanded as she toppled into his arms.

'I've come to return your briefcase.' Georgia gasped.

The muscles of his chest were hard against hers. With a singular lack of gallantry he pushed her away from him.

'I'm on a conference call.'

It was then Georgia noticed he was clutching a telephone and the strange buzzing in her ears was actually voices down the line demanding to know what was going on.

'You'd better come in.'

Dominic turned away from Georgia, leaving her to follow him into the room. She stood helplessly by his bed while he paced to and fro, the floorboards creaking in protest from the increased activity. The telephone exchange grew more heated.

Georgia had never stayed at The Duck, but she had been upstairs before when called upon to collect fares or help passengers with their bags.

As with all the rooms, Dominic's was low beamed and cramped. The floors were uneven and all the windows were diamond patterned, in keeping with the original appearance of The Duck. Over the years renovations had been carried out and the resultant mix match of styles and fashions added to the charm of what was originally a fifteenth century coaching inn.

Doing her best not to listen to what Dominic was saying, Georgia fiddled with the belt tied around the briefcase. She tried to tighten it, but her efforts only made things worse and moments later it unravelled itself. The lock was loose, too, and the lid flew open, spilling the contents out on to the floor.

Dominic turned round at the sound of the disturbance behind him.

'Sorry,' Georgia apologised in a whisper as she scooped up the papers and tried to put them back into some order. 'The catch gave way.'

'Leave it,' Dominic ordered. 'I'll get back to you.'

Cutting off his call he snatched back the files and taking the briefcase from Georgia, he rammed them back inside.

For a moment the two of them glared at each other. Georgia did her best to control her heavy breathing and wished she had thought to smarten up before attempting to deliver Dominic's brief-case back to him. Her hair, she knew, was in sore need of attention and her jacket smelled strongly of damp dog.

Dominic's nostrils twitched. Georgia flushed.

'Sorry. I'm in my dog-walking clothes,' she said in an attempt to explain her dishevelled state.

Dominic's deep-set clear blue eyes did not waver as he took in every detail of her appearance.

'So you found it?' He spoke first. 'My briefcase,' he added as Georgia frowned at him in confusion.

'Yes,' she pulled herself together, remembering why she was here. 'One of my drivers told me how you like to put a high-visibility strap on your luggage for easy identification. Your case was in the office all the time.'

Georgia wasn't sure whether or not her explanation was making sense but there was something about the way Dominic was looking at her that was unnerving.

'Mix-ups would seem to be something you do rather well, wouldn't you say?' His smile did not reach his eyes.

'I can only apologise on behalf of Georgia Cabs,' Georgia did her best to retrieve the situation, 'but I can assure you no-one interfered with the contents of your case.'

'Except you.' Dominic looked down to where a stray sheet of paper had escaped their attention. He picked it up.

'That was an accident. I'm sorry.' Georgia was not used to apologising so often and knew her colour was rising. She would have liked to point out that some of the responsibility for the initial error rested with Dominic himself, but he didn't look to be in the mood to be reminded of that fact.

'How did you get in here? I gave orders at the desk that they were to let no-one up.'

'It wasn't the front desk's fault. They said you weren't staying here, but I knew you were because I recognised the telephone number you gave me. Then I saw your room number was written on the back of your card.'

'That was careless of me,' he admitted. 'So displaying a casual disregard for my specific instructions that no-one was to be admitted, you decided to make your own way to my room?'

'You left me in no doubt that the return of your briefcase was top priority,' Georgia flared back at him. 'I seem to remember you threatening to sue us if we didn't find it.' There was only so much of his attitude she could take and her patience was wearing thin. 'So now I have returned your property to you, I trust there's nothing else to detain me, unless of course you were planning to have me clapped in irons?'

She knew the last remark bordered on unprofessional, but it slipped out before Georgia could stop herself.

'I don't think there's any need to go that far — yet,' Dominic said, the suggestion of reluctant respect softening the weathered features of his face.

Georgia was the first to look away.

'Right, well, I'll be off,' she said.

'I hope you weren't followed up here.'

The scar on Dominic's forehead seemed more pronounced as his smile turned to a frown. 'The bar is full of journalists.'

'That's why I couldn't telephone you from the desk,' Georgia explained. 'The receptionist wouldn't put me through and I didn't dare use my mobile in case someone overheard.'

There was another discreet tap on the door.

'It seems someone else may have got past this receptionist,' Dominic said, raising his eyebrows.

Georgia began to feel uncomfortable. She didn't want to be found in Dominic's room. If it should be a journalist they might put the wrong interpretation on her presence here.

'Perhaps I'd better leave,' she suggested.

'Perhaps you had,' he agreed, 'and thank you for this.' He nodded at the briefcase.

As Dominic opened the door to the newcomer, his knee buckled, causing his foot to slip. Georgia tripped over his cargo boot and for the second time Dominic put out his arms to catch her.

Standing in the corridor was a stunning beautiful girl, with long blonde hair and the most perfect complexion Georgia had ever seen in her life.

'Er.' Georgia tried to wriggle out of

Dominic's hold. 'I was just leaving.'

'Not a moment too soon,' the girl replied, her eyes as cold as chips of ice, 'but before you go I would be interested to hear what you are doing in my fiancé's bedroom with your arms around his neck.'

A Face From the Past

'Hello, Belle.' Dominic greeted the girl with an easy smile. Georgia's attempt to release herself from Dominic's hold proved futile as he tightened his arms around her waist. Short of being undignified, there was nothing Georgia could do but succumb to his hold and try to talk her way out of what had to be the most embarrassing situation of her life.

'Dominic,' Belle challenged him with her deep violet eyes, 'if this is an attempt to make me jealous then really.' Her lip curled as she took in Georgia's dishevelled appearance. 'You are going to have to do better.'

'If I could just put a word in edgewise,' Georgia began.

'Who exactly are you?' Belle asked, not looking too interested in anything Georgia might have to say.

'Actually,' Dominic admitted with a

rueful smile at Georgia, 'I don't know your name. You never got round to introducing yourself.'

'Georgia Jones,' she mumbled.

'Goodness, with a name like that she sounds like a cow girl,' Belle trilled at Dominic, revealing cosmetically enhanced teeth, 'and if I may say so,' she turned her attention back to Georgia 'your appearance is a bit Calamity Jane, too. Are you a reporter or one of those dreadful girls that will keep chasing poor old Dom all over the place? We have such trouble fighting them off, don't we, darling?'

'Georgia is a cab driver,' Dominic clipped back at her. 'Georgia, meet Belle Jeffreys. She's a friend.' He lingered over his choice of word to describe their relationship.

Seizing her moment, Georgia delivered a sharp jab in his ribs with her elbows. He yelped and she managed to wriggle free from his hold.

'I can speak up for myself, thank you. I haven't yet lost the power of speech.'

'I wasn't suggesting you had,' he

replied, 'and did you have to give me such a vicious dig?'

Ignoring his look of discomfort Georgia addressed herself to Belle. 'Miss Jeffreys,' she began.

'I prefer Ms,' Belle replied.

'Ms Jeffreys.' Georgia attempted to soften her words with a smile then drawing on her driver's diplomacy skills and refusing to be intimidated by Belle's superior expression said, 'I was in Mr Talbot's room for a very valid reason.'

'I don't know how you managed to worm your way past reception. Dominic, I should speak to the manager. Didn't you tell them there were to be no callers?'

'I did,' Dominic confirmed, 'but Ms Jones seems to have exercised a remarkable degree of initiative and found her way up here. By the way, how did you get past security?'

'When you're as well-known as I am all doors are open to you,' Belle replied.

Georgia frowned. Now she came to look at her properly, there was something familiar about the girl's face.

'Are you an actress?' she asked. 'Haven't I seen you in that soap opera about a zoo?'

Dominic hastily turned his amusement into a cough, signifying an apology with his hands. The moment Georgia finished her question she could see she had said the wrong thing.

'I never act with children or animals,' Belle replied.

'You don't do much acting at all at the moment, do you?' Dominic butted in. 'Aren't you resting?'

'I'm in talks with my agent.' Belle creamy complexion was now stained an angry shade of pink.

'Of course you are. Well lovely as it is to see you, Ms Jones and I were on our way out for something to eat. So if you don't mind? We are running late.'

'I don't care who you take out to dinner. In fact, I don't care if I never see you again.'

Appalled Georgia watched Belle flounce off down the corridor.

'Go after her,' she urged Dominic

delivering another blow to his chest. Dominic staggered against the door-frame.

'I wish you'd stop doing that. I shall be covered in bruises in the morning.'

'Don't you care that your fiancée has just walked out of your life?'

'She isn't my fiancée. She isn't even my girlfriend. We've been out socially a couple of times but that's the full extent of our relationship.'

'Ms Jeffreys seems to think differently.'

'Ms Jeffreys is seeking to further her career and, like everyone else round here, present company excepted, she seems to be more interested in my work than me. Now about that dinner date.'

'I'm not having supper with you,' Georgia protested.

'You know I'm going to get a complex about the number of girls walking out on me,' Dominic complained. 'My pride is in danger of being seriously wounded.'

'I'm sure you can hack it and, if you

can remember, I came here to return your briefcase, which I have done. I have no intention of getting involved in your private life. Now if you'll excuse me I have to get back to Den.'

'Who is Den?'

'The sous chef. I promised Patsy a walk by the river.'

'I'm afraid you've lost me there.' Dominic looked perplexed. 'You're going for a walk by the river with the sous chef who's called Patsy?'

'No. Den is looking after Patsy for me. Patsy and I are going for a walk. She's my dog.'

'So I won't be playing gooseberry if I tag along?'

'No.'

It wasn't what Georgia had meant to say but her head was buzzing and she was finding it difficult to concentrate.

'Good.' Dominic grabbed up a leather jacket. 'In that case shall we sneak out the fire exit?'

Before Georgia could think up another excuse she and Dominic were moments later inching their way down the iron staircase.

'Good grief!' Den nearly jumped out of his skin as Patsy, catching sight of her mistress, began barking and running round in excited circles. 'Where did you spring from?'

'Den, is it?' Dominic smiled at him. 'How do you do? I'm Dominic Talbot.'

'I know who you are.' Den got to his feet. 'I didn't realise you were staying here.'

'Strictly speaking, I'm not,' Dominic replied. 'Can I rely on you to keep that bit of information to yourself?'

'Den knows how to be discreet,' Georgia snapped. Now she'd got her breath back she was annoyed at the way she had been manipulated into creeping out of the back entrance of The Duck. 'Thanks, Den. Hope Patsy wasn't too much trouble.'

'Hey, where are you going?' Dominic called out as Georgia scooped up Patsy and began walking to her cab.

'I don't think that's any of your

business, do you?' Georgia unlocked her cab door.

'Mr Talbot,' The cry went up from one of the journalists who had slipped outside into the car park to see if anything was going on. 'Dominic.'

'I'd get moving if I were you, sir,' Den advised him. 'I'll hold him off for as long as I can.'

'Thanks, Den. I owe you one.'

Before Georgia could protest Dominic jumped into her passenger seat.

'Drive,' he instructed her.

'How dare you barge your way into my vehicle?' she began.

'This is a cab, isn't it?'

'Yes,' Georgia began.

'Then I'm hiring you. I'll pay you the appropriate fare. Get a move on.'

Catching sight of several more journalists who appeared to have taken up the call Georgia started her engine.

'Where do you want me to take you?'

'Didn't you tell me Patsy needs exercise?' He gestured to the reporters. 'Let's head for the river.'

'I'm not really dressed for somewhere as smart as Jean Pierre's,' Georgia told him as they strolled back along the towpath, picking their way carefully through the long grass. The light had faded from the day and it was difficult to see where the path dipped. 'That's if you could get a table at such short notice,' she added.

When Georgia had protested that she couldn't accepted the generous fare Dominic offered her, he suggested he make a contribution to the charity her parents had nominated for the summer season. Unable to decline his offer, Georgia could think of no further reason to refuse to have supper with him if they found somewhere that would take dogs.

'At the moment Patsy's left alone during the day,' she explained. 'When my parents are here there's always someone around to walk her, but there's only me while they're away. That's why I like to spend as much spare time with her as possible.'

'Leave things to me,' Dominic replied as he hurriedly made a telephone call.

Georgia watched the gnats darting around on the night air promising another fine day.

'All settled,' Dominic replied. 'If we're prepared to eat outside. Don't worry. They assure me the patio is heated and well-behaved dogs are allowed in the garden.'

They were the only two diners on the terrace and Jean-Pierre seated them at a table set for four.

'Everyone seems to prefer eating inside tonight,' he explained. 'There were rumours of rain, but it has, I think, passed. Now can I tempt you to my dish of the day? Grilled sea bass, green salad and new potatoes, with perhaps to follow a slice of my special raspberry tart?'

'Sounds delicious.'

'Who is the driver?' Jean-Pierre asked.

'I am.'

'Then for you a glass of freshly squeezed orange juice.'

'I'll have the same,' Dominic replied.

'I need to keep a clear head for tomorrow morning's meetings.'

'Ah yes, the famous costume drama.' Jean-Pierre smiled. 'I hear nothing else for days. Do you have a part for a drop-dead-gorgeous Frenchman?'

Dominic raised an eyebrow at Georgia. 'You're not after a starring role, too, are you?'

She shuddered. 'I'm definitely a back room girl.'

'Pity. Good lighting could turn your complexion to porcelain.'

'What about me? I asked first.' Jean-Pierre butted in, saving Georgia's blushes.

'Sorry, Jean-Pierre. Don't call us, we'll call you.'

The Frenchman shrugged and patted his ample stomach. 'Maybe you are right. I leave playing the hero to the younger men. Now, I will personally see to your order.'

He bustled away and a silence fell between Georgia and Dominic. Through the open doors Georgia could hear the sound of the other diners talking and a piano playing discreet music in the background.

'What shall we talk about?' Dominic asked, attacking the basket of bread Jean-Pierre had placed on the table.

Georgia wished he wouldn't look at her so intently. There was something unnerving about the expression in his clear blue eyes.

'You choose,' she said as she nibbled on an olive.

'Are you a local girl?' Dominic asked. 'That's always a good starter.'

'Born and bred,' Georgia replied. 'Although my grandmother was Russian.'

'What was she doing over here, your grandmother?'

'She never talked much about her past but my grandfather told me they met when she was eighteen. He said her family were quite wealthy and wanted her to learn English so she took a job as lady's companion. My grandfather was the family chauffeur. They met and they fell in love.'

'That's quite some story,' Dominic said.

'I don't know the details but soon after the marriage my grandmother lost both her parents so she never did return to her homeland. Anyway, there you have it, a potted family history. My grandmother was the driving force behind Georgia Cabs. It was she who first set up a small business with my grandfather. I think he had ideas of taking up painting for a living, but nothing came of it. I inherited his love of art but I couldn't make a living at it, either, so here I am.'

'And it was from your grandmother that you inherited your stubborn willpower?'

'I'm not stubborn,' insisted Georgia, then, catching the teasing glint in Dominic's eyes, admitted with a self-conscious smile, 'sometimes it's the only way to get things done.'

'And the art that you couldn't make a living at?'

'I had a year in Florence. I met an Italian called Carlo. He took me everywhere on his little scooter and showed me all the sights. After twelve months my parents insisted I came home and did some proper work. Now it's your turn.'

'There's not much to tell really. My father was a lodge porter at a minor college. He knew lots of academic types, always with their noses in a book. I think that's where I got my love of the written word. I was always good at making up stories. Actually I can remember the incident that started me off. Several of the tutors did tours as trained guides and I used to like listening to them. You know the sort of thing?'

'William Shakespeare slept here?' Georgia suggested.

'Something along those lines. Anyway, one day I took a friend's place as guide on a tour of the college and what I didn't know I sort of invented.'

Georgia's eyes widened. 'Were you ever found out?'

'Not by my father, thanks goodness. The tourists all enjoyed it and I had a great evening. They even took me out for a meal afterwards and eating and drinking was something I did know about, so a good time was had by all. Here's our meal and not a moment too soon.' Dominic squirted lemon juice on his sea bass. 'Much more of your interrogation techniques and I would have confessed all my sins.'

They ate for a few moments in silence.

'Glad to see you've got a healthy appetite,' Dominic looked approvingly at her plate. 'Most of the actresses I mix with are on some sort of diet or suffer allergies.'

'I don't have time to be allergic to anything,' Georgia said, 'and I only had a tube of fruit gums for lunch.'

'They'll ruin your teeth.'

'Lately my life's been too hectic to cook.'

'I'm sorry I was short with you about my briefcase,' Dominic said as Georgia finished the last of her fish. 'I've got a lot riding on this latest venture and I could see months of work going down the drain. It was my fault for leaving it in the cab. I know I should make back-up copies of my work, but when I'm on a roll I always forget about it, and even when I do make copies I leave memory sticks all over the place. When you said you'd found my bag I was so relieved. It was a double blow when I thought you'd lost it again. Shall we say my artistic temperament got the better of me?'

'Apology accepted,' Georgia replied. 'We do our best to reunite our passengers with their belongings, but you'd be amazed what gets left behind in cabs and sometimes people insist it's not theirs.'

'Really? I had no idea lost property was such a delicate science.'

'So this is where you hang out these days?' A voice behind Georgia interrupted them. 'I must say you've moved up market, Georgia. Raspberry tarts at Jean-Pierre's. You're charging too much for those taxi rides of yours.' There was another pause. 'Dominic Talbot, isn't it?'

Georgia spun round.

'You have the advantage of me, I'm afraid.' Dominic looked up at the new arrival.

'Max Doyle.' He introduced himself easily.

'I don't believe we've met, have we?'

'I'm Georgia's fiancé, or I thought I was.'

Dominic raised an eyebrow as he looked at Georgia for an explanation.

'Max is not my fiancé,' she ground at him through gritted teeth. 'He isn't even my boyfriend.'

'Slight misunderstanding.' Max's smile didn't slip.

'Not on my part.' Georgia glared at him. 'Now if you don't mind I'd like to finish my raspberry tart.'

* * *

'You've really fallen on your feet,' Max said with the easy smile he always used to charm important people as he looked round the private office Georgia was using in her father's absence. 'Running the show by yourself. I'm impressed.'

Georgia stirred milk into the coffee and passed a mug over to him. Max tasted it and grimaced. 'Don't you offer your clients freshly ground coffee?'

'Sorry, our customers are busy people. They don't have time to sit around all day drinking coffee and neither do the staff,' Georgia snapped, annoyed that yet another man had inveigled her into giving him a lift.

Max had insisted they drop Dominic off first at The Duck before coming back to the Georgia Cabs control centre.

'By the fire exit will do,' Dominic said from the back seat. 'One of the chamber maids lives in and she's promised to open it for me.'

'Very cloak and dagger,' drawled Max. 'What it is to be famous.'

In the darkness of the cab he didn't see the furious look Georgia threw at him.

'Bye, Georgia.' Dominic opened the door quietly after making sure there were no reporters lurking in the bushes. 'Thanks for everything. I do appreciate it. Max.' He nodded at him, but said nothing more.

'Where's your car?' Georgia demanded, turning to Max as the fire exit door opened for Dominic and he disappeared inside The Duck.

'I booked a taxi for my dinner date,' Max made an embarrassed face, 'with New Cabs, actually. Sorry about that.' Georgia refused to rise to his bait. 'After I arrived at Jean-Pierre's I got a message to say my contact had been unavoidably delayed and could we re-schedule? I was texting for a cab when I caught sight of you sitting out on the terrace, so I decided to join you.'

'Why?'

'I'd had a couple of glasses of wine in the bar while I was waiting for my dinner date.'

Georgia frowned. 'I still don't follow you.'

'We need to talk and I thought tonight would be as good an opportunity as ever,' Max said by way of explanation.

'I think we've said everything that needs to be said, don't you?' Georgia replied.

'Did you get my letter?' Max asked, easing back in his chair, looking totally relaxed.

'Yes.'

Max waited as if expecting Georgia to elaborate. When she didn't he asked, 'Aren't you going to ask me what happened to Kelly?'

'Max.' Georgia leaned forward, 'I'm glad you managed to track me down this evening.'

The beginnings of a knowing smile crossed Max's face. 'Thought so,' he said.

'Because it saved me the trouble of contacting you.'

'I knew you'd understand about me and Kelly.'

Max's arrogance almost caused Georgia to lose the thread of what she had been about to say.

'I am not interested in your relationship with Kelly. Neither am I interested in rekindling my relationship with you.'

'You don't mean that,' Max continued smiling.

'I can assure you I do.'

'All proper relationships suffer setbacks.'

'This was more than a setback. We were engaged.'

'I'll admit I behaved badly, but it won't happen again, I promise.'

'It won't happen again because I won't give you the chance,' Georgia replied firmly. 'Now can I get one of my drivers to give you a lift to the station?'

'You don't seem to understand.' Max showed no signs of moving on. 'And you needn't think pretending to be an item with Dominic Talbot will work. I happen to know his interests are otherwise engaged.'

'I've already told you I don't need to understand about you and Kelly because my life has moved on.'

'Actually I am not talking about Kelly.'

'What are you talking about, then?' Georgia was losing interest in the conversation. She began to scan the week's figures and noted with satisfaction an increase in bookings over the previous week.

'I'm talking about Dod Manor.'

Georgia looked up sharply.

'I thought that would catch your attention,' Max said with a complacent smile.

'Dod Manor?'

'Exactly.' Max adjusted the cuff of his business shirt. For the first time Georgia realised he was wearing the suit he always chose for meetings, coupled with a white shirt and dark tie. For a Sunday evening it was rather a formal dress code. 'As I've already explained I was due to meet a contact this evening before he was forced to cry off.'

'Go on,' Georgia said reluctantly.

'Dod Manor has been purchased by a syndicate of which I am a significant shareholder.'

'You've bought the Manor?'

'I have the senior stake in it, yes. My partners and I plan to completely refurbish it then see in what direction our business venture can take us. That means I shall be visiting Dod Stretton a lot more frequently, especially as we have our first commission before we've done a thing to the place.'

'Then it's true?'

'I presume you are referring to the proposed filming of a costume drama? Yes.'

'Surely Dod Manor won't pass the latest health and safety requirements?'

'All the shots will be taken outside. The gardens are, I admit, overgrown, but a competent team of landscapers will be able to lick them into shape before filming starts. I don't understand these things but I gather the cameras can angle shots at the house to show it in its best light. The fee being offered is substantial and will make a major contribution towards our renovation costs.'

Georgia blinked at Max, uncertain what to say. Of course the development would provide an injection of funds into the local economy and she knew she should be pleased, but a part of her couldn't help wishing Max wasn't so closely involved in the project.

'Well, that is good news.' She forced herself to smile.

'I thought you would be pleased,' Max replied. 'There will be extra work for you. I have actually already approached New Cabs and they seem keen on offering us special rates.'

'Us?'

'The team. I'll introduce you to everyone when things are up and running. At the moment you can imagine we are in a state of flux. To be honest we didn't expect an approach this soon and it's rather caught us on the hop. We haven't even officially designed our website so it was a bit of a coup.'

'If there is anything Georgia Cabs can do to help,' Georgia began, 'we would be only too pleased.'

She was more than aware that Max was capable of playing her off against

New Cabs and that was a scenario she was anxious to avoid. All the same it would be counter productive to let their personal history stand in the way of new business.

'Naturally our past relationship . . . '

'Will have nothing to do with the present,' Georgia said firmly.

'I only thought . . . ' Max began again.

'I am not your fiancée any more, Max and I would be grateful if you would refrain from giving people that impression.'

'Surely you're not going to let that interlude with Kelly colour what we have between us?'

'We have nothing between us apart from a business connection.'

Max's eyes narrowed. 'I would suggest you don't make any hasty decisions.'

Georgia could feel her sea bass churning in her stomach. Max, she knew, was ruthless when it came to business deals. He thrived on the cut and thrust of high-powered commercial decisions.

'I wouldn't like to think you were blackmailing me into anything.' Georgia decided to call his bluff.

Underneath the confident exterior Max was at heart a bully and the only way to deal with a bully, in Georgia's experience, was to stand up to them.

'Goodness, nothing so grubby.' Max made a placatory gesture with his hands.

'I'm pleased to hear it.' Georgia smiled. 'I'm sure the other members of your syndicate wouldn't wish to be associated with anything — grubby.'

Max paled under his tan. Georgia hoped whatever plan he had in mind had been successfully nipped in the bud.

'Now, if you're not going to finish your coffee can one of my drivers take you anywhere?'

'Is there any chance you could fix me a sandwich? I've eaten hardly a thing all day.'

'Certainly.' Georgia turned to the small fridge she kept in a corner of the office, opened it and, producing a filling station sandwich, passed it across the desk to Max. 'It's a day old, I'm afraid, but it should still be fresh. I didn't get time to eat it earlier.'

Wrinkling his nose at the strong aroma of stale cheese, Max said, 'Thanks, I'll pass.'

Georgia did her best not to smile. It was never a wise idea to think you had got the better of Max Doyle.

Accepting defeat, he stood up. 'Don't worry about that lift, either. I'll telephone New Cabs. I'm sure they'll be happy to oblige.'

'I'm sure they will,' Georgia replied, hoping she hadn't overstepped the mark.

'I'll see myself out.'

Max could be ruthless with those who crossed him. She'd seen what he was capable of when he was in danger of having his plans thwarted. He was proud of his reputation as one of the local businessmen of the year and personal issues would not be allowed to get in the way of his professional ambition.

The telephone on her desk signalled an incoming personal call. Unused to receiving calls on her private line so late in the day and hoping it wasn't an emergency she picked it up.

'Hello?'

'Georgia?'

Her mouth dried at the sound of Dominic's voice.

'Yes. Er, you got back to your room OK?'

'No problem,' he assured her.

A silence fell between them as she waited for him to tell her the reason for his call.

'I wanted to apologise.'

'For what?'

'If I caused problems between you and your,' he paused, 'fiancé?' he queried.

'I am not engaged to Max Doyle.'

The night shift operator looked up, startled by the sound of her raised voice. She signalled through the glass window that everything was fine.

'That's not the impression he gave.'

'We were engaged but,' Georgia hesitated, 'we broke it off.'

'Right. You know he's a member of the syndicate involved in the proposed Dod Manor development? I've seen his name on the paperwork.'

'Max told me tonight.'

'I wouldn't want to think I'd jeopardised things on that front by inviting you out to dinner.'

'I don't think even Max could sway the syndicate to that extent,' Georgia replied. 'Our relationship was personal and nothing to do with his business affairs.'

'Glad to hear it. Everyone's got a lot riding on this deal.' Dominic lapsed into silence.

'Was there anything else?' Georgia asked eventually.

'No, just thanks for not telling the press I was holed up here. Can I ring you next time I'm in the area?'

'Georgia Cabs will always be pleased to hear from you.'

'I wasn't actually talking about taxis.'

Georgia was surprised to find her face felt hot. 'I, er, weren't you?'

'In these days of equal rights you could, of course, invite me out to dinner. I wouldn't say no,' he added with a smile in his voice.

'Wouldn't you?'

Since her break-up with Max, Georgia had only been out with Jake and that was on a very casual basis. Unused to this type of conversation with a man, she lapsed into silence.

'Sweet dreams,' Dominic said in a voice that sent shivers down her spine.

As Georgia replaced the receiver, Jake poked his head round the door.

'Was that Max Doyle I saw outside just now getting into one of Dad's cabs?' he asked.

'Yes, it was.' Georgia looked up.

'What's he doing back here?' Jake asked with a frown.

'I think,' Georgia spoke carefully, 'we are going to have to steel ourselves to seeing a lot more of Max Doyle in the coming weeks.'

'Thanks For Rescuing Me'

The following few days passed in a flurry of activity. Georgia had no time to think about Max or Dominic due to the increased workload. New Cabs, it seemed, had over-stretched their facilities and were unable to meet all their commitments and Georgia was pleased to find several old customers returning to the fold.

'So, it's not a rumour any more.'

Jake produced a copy of the local newspaper late one afternoon and tapped a fingernail on the headlines. Underneath was a provocative picture of Belle Jeffreys wearing a huge straw hat, a vibrant poppy patterned shirt and tight white slacks. She had, it seemed, won the lead role in the costume drama over fierce competition from other actresses.

'I can't wait to start filming,' Belle gushed to the reporter, 'I admire

Dominic Talbot's work tremendously. He is a major talent and it will be an honour and privilege to work with him.'

Georgia hid a wry smile as she wondered what Dominic would make of the interview. Much of the rest of the story Georgia already knew, but along with everyone else she was surprised at the speed with which things were now moving. Every day saw the arrival of another contractor at the manor. Village stalwarts were forming focus groups to ensure the tranquillity of Dod Stretton was not compromised.

'I drove past Dod Manor the other day,' one of Georgia's female drivers informed her, 'and you should see what they've done to the grounds.' She gave a shamefaced smile. 'I must admit I parked up on the verge and had a good peer through the railings.'

'What did you see?' Jake asked.

'They've cut back all the wilderness and there's a lawn laid out, and I think they're building a water feature of some sort and one of those Grecian summer house things. It looks really lovely.'

'I hope you didn't abandon your fare,' Georgia cautioned her.

'Of course I didn't. Don't worry, Georgia, your team won't let you down.'

'Everything's all right, isn't it?' Jake asked with a concerned frown after the driver had strolled away. 'It's unlike you to be snappy and you know you can trust everyone to behave professionally.'

'Sorry,' Georgia apologised. 'All this extra business is a bit of a headache when it comes to paperwork, that's all.'

'You know where to come for a shoulder to cry on,' Jake offered, blushing as he remembered his father's advice. Whilst he wasn't totally on side with all his father's views, becoming more than good friends with Georgia was something they did agree on.

'Thanks. I'll bear it in mind.'

'By the way, don't forget it's quiz night tonight at The Duck. Try not to let us down again.'

'I'll do my best,' Georgia promised.

Back in her office she sat quietly for a

few moments and tried to compose her thoughts. She couldn't shake off the feeling that, given the chance, Max Doyle would cause mischief. He hadn't liked it when she had broken off their engagement and if he thought there was anything between herself and Dominic Talbot, he was more than capable of stirring things up.

'Georgia?' Ray signalled through from the control centre. 'Personal call on line one.'

She waved back at him and picked up her extension.

'Georgia Jones speaking. How may I help you?'

'By providing me with a cab. I have been waiting at the station for over half-an-hour, but New Cabs seem to have forgotten I exist.'

'Dominic?' Her heart leapt at the sound of his voice, then remembering her professionalism, replied, 'I'll just see if we have a driver free.'

'I want you.'

'Sorry?'

'You do drive?'

'On occasions, yes.'

Georgia glanced at the wall clock. It was late in the day and several of her female drivers had clocked off to fetch children from their various after-school activities. She doubted they would be able to meet Dominic's request unless she called a driver in.

'Where do you want to go?'

'Stretton Wood.'

'What on earth for?' The question was out before Georgia could stop herself. 'Sorry,' she apologised, 'it's none of my business.'

'You're right, it isn't,' Dominic replied, 'but I'm willing to discuss anything you like as long as it's from the inside of a cab. I'll see you in five.'

'Ray,' Georgia called out as she shrugged on the jacket she kept for occasions such as these. It was pale blue wool and, coupled with her tailored trousers, passed as a presentable uniform that usually fitted most occasions.

'Problem?'

'Special request from a passenger. What's free?'

'Nothing.' He looked down at his list.

'We always have one or two cabs on the forecourt.'

'Not today, we don't,' he paused 'apart from number six.'

'Is there anything wrong with number six?'

'Engine keeps cutting out. Jake reported it last week. It's booked into the garage tomorrow.'

'Give me the key.'

'Are you sure?' Ray looked doubtful.

'It's either number six or we leave Dominic Talbot stranded at the station.'

'He wasn't one of ours, was he?' Ray asked in concern.

'No, New Cabs let him down.'

'In that case.' Ray handed over the key with a beaming smile. 'Here you are. Any problems, I'm on duty until seven. Want me to give Patsy her early evening walk?'

'Please.'

Ray was one of the few members of

staff she trusted to look after Patsy.

The cab purred along the lane on its way to the station and showed no sign of its recent temperament. A light shower had dampened the foliage and Georgia inhaled the deep green smell of the hawthorn.

Georgia swung the car into the station car park. Dominic was pacing to and fro in front of the squat red-bricked building and busy punching numbers into a mobile phone. He was wearing a leather jacket and cargo pants, the pockets bulging with what looked like pads of paper and millions of pencils. He glanced up at the sound of tyres on the forecourt and, snatching up his overnight bag, strode towards Georgia.

'Remind me to cancel the contract with New Cabs,' was the only greeting he gave Georgia as he folded his large frame into the passenger seat.

'I'm afraid I can't do that,' she admitted.

'Why not?' His blue eyes glared at her.

'As you pointed out, your contract is with New Cabs.'

'Only because that wretched syndicate headed up by your boyfriend recommended them.'

'Max is not my boyfriend,' Georgia said, her jaw tightening.

'Sorry.' Dominic now threw her a dazzling smile. 'I shouldn't be having a go at you. Thanks for rescuing me. I didn't know who else to call.'

'All part of the service,' Georgia relaxed and returned his smile. 'So Stretton Wood, sir?'

'The director wants to set a love scene there. I need to get a feel of the place.'

'It's quite a way out.'

'You're not in any hurry, are you?' Dominic asked.

Georgia glanced at the clock on the dashboard, remembering her promise to Jake. 'It is quiz night at The Duck.'

'Great.' Dominic did up his seat belt. 'I'll join you when we're through. I'm a wizard on films of the Sixties and

Seventies and vintage motorcycles. Any good to you?'

'All players welcome,' Georgia replied.

The cab seemed reluctant to re-start. Holding her breath, Georgia turned the key again and the engine sprang into life.

'Thought we had a problem for a moment there,' Dominic let out a sigh of relief as they moved forward. 'So, how are you?' He stretched out his long legs as he settled down.

'Fine.'

'Sorry I haven't been in touch. Life has been a bit hectic as you can imagine.'

'Are you allowed to talk about the production?' Georgia asked.

'There's not much to tell, really. It's the usual pre-shoot chaos at the moment. Everyone thinks filming is glamorous, but it's hard work.'

'Getting paid for dressing up and learning a few lines? Doesn't sound like hard work to me.'

'It's not much fun standing about in

a muddy field on a freezing morning, trying to pretend it's a sunny afternoon and everyone's having a lovely time.'

'Do writers have to do that?'

'I do.'

'I see your girlfriend has been cast as the female lead.'

Dominic threw Georgia a sideways glance.

'Belle is not my girlfriend,' he said in a low, clear voice.

'Sorry,' Georgia replied. 'Slip of the tongue.'

Dominic did not look convinced. 'I suppose I asked for that. What say we forget about Belle and Max?'

'Good idea,' Georgia agreed.

'Is it far to this Stretton Wood?' Dominic asked as they drove along.

'About three miles.'

'It's a bit of a local beauty spot, isn't it?'

'There's quite a lot of history attached to it.'

'I've been researching it on the net. What's all this about a tree?'

'The Stretton Oak?'

'That's the one.'

'The story goes way back. If you look hard enough they say you can still see the initials *E* and *W* carved in the bark.'

'E and W?'

'They stand for Eleanor and William.'

'Who were they?'

'Lady Eleanor was the daughter of the local lord of the manor. William was a brave warrior.'

'I suppose they fell in love but were torn apart?'

'Don't be like that,' Georgia protested.

'Sorry, you're talking to a world weary scriptwriter who's heard it all before. Go on,' Dominic urged.

'William was not of the nobility and Eleanor's father forbade them to marry. They decided to elope but Sir John found out about their plans and lured William to the forest with a false love note supposedly from his daughter. He forced William to fight a duel for the honour of Eleanor's hand. William was a younger, fitter man and it was obvious he could easily win, but out of respect for the older man he let Sir John have the day.'

'Poor old William.' Dominic began to look interested. 'You mean this Sir John killed him?'

'Eleanor was distraught at the news and her father was full of remorse. He tried to make amends, but one night Eleanor, unable to live with her grief, drowned herself in the river. Sir John wasn't given the chance to explain that William was, in fact, still alive.'

'So he didn't kill him?'

'No. Sir John, respecting William's noble gesture, banished him from the kingdom in exchange for his life.'

'They had it tough in those days, didn't they?' Dominic smiled. 'Still it's all grist to my writers' mill.'

'I haven't finished.'

'There's more?'

'William returned disguised as a woodman. When he learned of Eleanor's fate he challenged Sir John to another duel and this time he showed him no mercy.'

'Now that is serious. You don't go round killing the big guy.'

'Exactly. Realising what he had done William also drowned himself in the river after carving the words *for ever* under their initials on the tree.'

'That's quite some story.'

'The legend has survived over the years, along with the oak. It has withstood storms and desecration and the story goes that if it were to be vandalised then destruction would follow.'

'And on summer nights the swaying of the leaves in the tree sounds like the whisperings of sweet words between the lovers?' Dominic suggested.

'Don't mock it. These old country tales have a funny way of coming true.'

'I believe you,' Dominic agreed. 'I've worked in enough out of the way places to learn not to scoff at local tradition. Is it much further?' he asked, looking out the window.

'About ten minutes.'

The car engine began to shudder. 'What's wrong?'

Georgia looked down at the controls. All the gauges were registering normal. 'Just a blip,' she reassured him.

'Is there anywhere you can park?' Dominic asked as they drove deeper into the wood, 'while I make some notes?'

'I can drop you here, drive on for a bit and turn the car round further on where there's a suitable turning space.'

'You won't abandon me, will you?' Dominic asked with a fake look of alarm. 'I wouldn't want the ghost of Sir John to mistake me for William and decide it's time for a bit of revenge.'

'Georgia Cabs never abandons its passengers,' Georgia assured him with a smile, adding, 'And don't be such a scaredy cat.'

'Right, well, here goes.' Dominic grabbed his camera and quantities of notebooks. 'See you shortly.'

At this time of the evening there were

no other cars parked at the beauty spot, which made it easier for her to manoeuvre.

Glancing at her watch, she decided to give Jake a quick call to tell him she'd be late arriving at The Duck and that Dominic would be joining them.

'Great,' Jake enthused after she explained the reason for their delay. 'See you . . . '

His voice faded as the signal died.

Putting her mobile back in her bag, Georgia turned the ignition key and tried to restart the cab. The engine was dead.

An Adventure

'Where've you been?' Dominic demanded as Georgia trudged back through the forest, the hems of her smart trousers now caked with moist mud. 'And where's the car?'

'It won't start.'

'What?'

'It's been playing up.'

'Then why on earth did you bring it?'

'It was the only cab available and I didn't want to let you down. Ray said I should be able to nurse it along, as it was only a local call out. It's booked into the garage tomorrow.'

'Do you have any idea what's wrong with it?'

'Could be dirty connections. I believe someone filled it up with peculiar petrol a while back and it seems to have affected its reliability.'

'Well I'm finished here, I'll see if I

can have a go. I've nursed enough old bangers back to life in my time. Hold that.'

Dominic thrust his file of notes at Georgia then slung his camera around his neck.

'Did you call anyone to come and have a look at it?'

'I was hoping you had a mobile phone. Mine died on me when I was talking to Jake. I phoned him to say we'd be a bit late for the quiz evening.'

Dominic felt in the pockets of his cargo pants. 'I think my phone must have fallen out into the foot well of the cab when I stretched my legs. Come on, let's get back to the cab.'

For a few moments the only sound they made was the squelching of their feet as they walked over the slippery leaves underfoot. They were both breathing hard from the effort of struggling to stand upright. Georgia would have liked to cling on to Dominic's arm but the deepening of the scar on his forehead as he concentrated on not loosing his footing gave him a slightly menacing air and convinced her it would not be a good idea. He was also, she noticed, limping.

Hoping she wouldn't fall over she battled on. Her court shoes, practical for the office, were not designed for tramping through damp undergrowth.

'Where did you say you parked?' Dominic asked as they emerged into the clearing.

'Here.' Georgia caught her breath, then looked round in stunned surprise. 'I left the car here.'

Dominic raised his eyebrows at the sound of panic in her voice.

'Are you sure?'

'There are the tyre marks where I turned round. Look.'

She pointed to some deep gouges in the mud.

'Well the car's not here now.' Dominic put down his camera. 'I presume it hasn't been towed away because you were illegally parked?'

'Of course not.'

'Did you lock it?'

Georgia raised a horrified hand to

her face. 'I've just remembered something.'

'Don't tell me you left the keys in the ignition?'

That was exactly what Georgia had done.

'I didn't think,' she admitted, more than aware of the serious lapse in her conduct.

After attempting to start the car for over half-an-hour she realised Dominic would begin to wonder where she was. She had leapt out without giving the keys a second thought.

'At this time of day the car should have been safe.'

'There are notices,' Dominic pointed one out. 'Look, here's one.' It was nailed to a wooden post. 'You must have walked right by it. See, it tells you not to leave valuables in your car, to secure your vehicle and that all personal items of property are the owner's own responsibility.' The blue eyes taunted hers. 'The wording's rather like the ones in the back of your cabs, isn't it?'

Twin spots of colour highlighted

Georgia's cheekbones and in any other circumstances she would have told Dominic Talbot exactly what she thought of his petty point scoring tactics. As it was she could only agree with every word he said.

'Someone must have managed to get it started and driven off in it.' Dominic was speaking again. 'So, the only solution is to walk.'

Georgia looked up at Dominic. She knew she should apologise to him but she didn't know how to start.

'I've been in worst spots,' he assured her, 'and we're not far from civilisation. Come on.' He held out a hand. 'I don't want you to think I'm being male sexist, but I think you'd better cling on to me.'

'I can manage,' Georgia insisted.

'Not if you lose your footing and sprain your ankle. I don't think I'm up to carrying a healthy girl like you all the way back to Dod Stretton.'

Reluctantly Georgia slipped her fingers into Dominic's hand. It was warm against hers.

'There, that's better, isn't it? Right, off we go.'

'I don't know how whoever took the car managed to start it without my hearing them.'

'Trees deaden noise.'

'But they didn't pass me, either.'

'That is strange,' Dominic agreed. 'You don't think Sir John learned to drive sometime over the last three hundred years, took his test and nicked your cab do you?'

Despite the tumult of emotions dancing inside her stomach, some of Georgia's anxiety relaxed. 'Right now I can't come up with a better explanation,' she had to admit.

Dominic's remark lightened the mood between them and by the time they reached the edge of the forest Georgia felt more up to facing the challenge in front of them.

'I've always liked this time of day.' Dominic stopped to admire the view. 'The bit where twilight hasn't quite kicked in.'

Georgia paused beside him. In the far distance she could see one or two lights twinkling.

'Is there anywhere en route that's got a telephone?' Dominic asked.

'There's The Highwayman,' Georgia said.

'What's that?'

'It's an inn. It's had a bit of a chequered history and always being bought up by new owners. I'm not really sure if it's occupied at the moment.'

'Any port in a storm.'

Dominic was still holding her hand. Georgia knew she should have told him that now they were on the flat she was quite capable of walking unaided, but the feel of his firm hand against hers provided much-needed comfort. Never one to shirk her responsibilities she didn't know how she was going to explain what had happened to the rest of the staff.

An image of Max Doyle flashed through her mind. He would not have been half as understanding as Dominic. Max regarded inefficiency as the worst kind of sin and made no allowance for mistakes, no matter the circumstances.

'Is that it?' Dominic pointed to a creaky inn sign showing a rather romantic image of a masked highwayman holding up a coach with a pistol. A blonde female was looking out of the coach with a look of terror on her face. 'It doesn't seem very busy.'

Dominic rattled the knocker. 'If anyone is on the premises we should be able to make ourselves understood,' he replied. 'Cheer up.' he took in the glum expression on Georgia's face. 'I was once lost in The Urals facing what I can only describe as a disreputable band of urban terrorists who were clearly in no mood to compromise. Life doesn't get much worse than that, I can tell you.'

'I don't think anyone's in.' Georgia peered through a dirty window. 'It's dark inside.'

'Hello,' Dominic bellowed through the letter-box. 'Anyone at home?'

The hairs on the back of Georgia's neck rose.

'Did you hear that?' she asked.

'I did.' Dominic pulled a face as a dog began to bark in a manner that suggested he was more than adept at dealing with trespassers. 'Bit undignified to leg it in the circumstances, though, wouldn't you say?'

Moments later there was the sound of heavy footsteps working their way down the corridor.

'Sorry to bother you,' Dominic shouted through the letter-box again, 'but we're stranded and we wondered if you had a telephone we could use.'

There was the noise of what sounded like half-a-dozen chains being undone then locks being turned before the door creaked open. Georgia moved closer to Dominic then felt a wild desire to laugh. The person who met her eyes was the sweetest little white-haired woman she had ever seen.

'I'm sorry, my dears,' she replied, 'my hearing isn't all it should be. If it hadn't been for Gulliver here barking, I wouldn't have known there was anyone outside. He barks extra loud to alert my attention and I'm not very quick on my feet. It takes me a while to get to the door.'

A pink tongue lolled out of the friendly canine face of the dog by her side.

'What can I do for you?'

'We're very sorry to disturb you, Mrs . . . ?'

'Green. Hilda Green.'

'My name is Dominic Talbot and this is my companion, Georgia Jones.'

Mrs Green peered at them over her bi-focals. 'You look rather muddy. Have you been in an accident?'

Georgia decided to take charge of the situation. 'We wondered if we could borrow your telephone.'

'I'm so sorry,' she began.

'We'll pay you back.' Georgia searched in her handbag for her wallet.

'It's not that, dear. I don't have a telephone.'

Dominic and Georgia gaped at her.

'I'm only house-sitting for the new

people, you see. They're not due for another week or so and the line hasn't been connected.'

'Surely you need some sort of emergency contact out here on your own.'

'I'm not on my own.' She smiled. 'I have Gulliver and the man from the village calls every day with supplies. Then there's my radio and the chickens.'

Dominic cast a sideways glance at Georgia as if at a loss as to how to go on.

'I know it's asking an awful lot of you, Mrs Green,' Georgia said.

'Call me Hilda, dear,' she insisted.

'Hilda. Do you think we could come in for a few moments?'

'Of course. You'll want to freshen up. I do have plenty of hot running water and I expect you'd like something to eat.'

'We wouldn't want to impose,' Dominic protested.

'There's a fire in the lounge. You can get warm there. Come on through.'

They ate a hearty stew in the dining-room. Mrs Green proved to be an excellent hostess, regaling them with tales of her house-sitting assignments and of the various places she had visited.

'After my husband died I was very lonely. We had no children, you see, so I decided to get myself a little job. It's been so interesting. I'm always bumping into people, like yourselves. People I would never have met had I stayed at home.'

'This is certainly a very different property to house-sit,' Georgia agreed, looking up at the wooden panels and the stuffed animal heads. They made her want to shiver.

'You feel it, too, don't you?' Mrs Green looked keenly at her.

'Sorry?'

'The atmosphere. The house gets very cold at night. That's why I light the fires. I was reading up about a duel fought in the forest. One of the men was supposed to have stayed here the night before he killed another man. Somebody important, I believe.'

Dominic cast Georgia a wry look and she wondered what his writer's mind was making of this one.

'Anyway, if you've finished, would you like some coffee by the fire in the lounge?'

'We really must be on our way,' Georgia insisted, not wanting to move an inch.

'Must you go?' Mrs Green looked disappointed. 'You would be doing me a great favour if you stayed over. It's very cosy in the snug. I can't offer you a bed for the night but there are some comfortable chairs and I've loads of blankets. Sorry. I am being silly.' She began to look flustered.

'Mrs Green, I mean Hilda,' Dominic asked in a gentle voice. 'Has there been some trouble?'

'Not really. Well, yes. I think I had intruders the other night. That's why the security company has put extra locks on the doors. They're due to send a man up tomorrow. It might only have been lads from the village, all the same after dark things get a bit more scary, don't they?'

'And you'd like some company tonight?' Dominic said.

'We'll stay,' Georgia insisted.

'I wouldn't want to put you out and, like I said, I can't provide a bed.'

'That doesn't matter. As long as we're warm,' Dominic put in.

'I'll sort out the coffee, Hilda. Why don't you and Gulliver sit by the fire?' Georgia suggested, getting to her feet.

'Will anyone be looking for you?' Georgia asked Dominic as they left Hilda snoozing in the lounge while they washed up in the kitchen.

'Not if I'm away for only the one night. What about you?'

'Patsy should be all right. Ray promised to walk her before he went off duty and I know he would see to her water and feed her for me. As for Jake, he'll probably think I've cried off the quiz night again. I have to report the loss of the cab, of course, but no-one will notice it's missing overnight, I don't think.'

'Sad, isn't it?' Dominic said.

'What's sad?'

'No-one will be looking for us.'

The snug was indeed very cosy. There were plenty of soft chairs and blankets and a blazing log fire. Georgia felt sleepy.

'What made you become a writer?' she asked as she sipped a glass of wine.

'I suppose growing up in the grounds of a university fired my imagination. There were some clever academic types around. What about you? How did you come to be running a cab firm?'

'My father runs it really, but he is looking to retire and I think my parents may move permanently to Australia if I make a success of things in their absence. That's where they are now, visiting my brother. I enjoy the work. I could never sit in an office all day. That's it really.'

Georgia's eyelids now began to droop.

'I suppose we should sort out some

sort of bedding arrangements,' Dominic stirred himself. 'I'll sleep in the dining-room.'

'Will you be comfortable enough?'

'I can sleep on a washing line.' Dominic shook out one of Hilda's blankets. 'When it comes to bedding I must say Hilda doesn't stint. These are enormous.'

He brushed his lips against her forehead. 'I'll have a quick scout round, make sure everything's locked up for the night. Fun, isn't it? Reminds me of my camping holidays when I was a boy.'

Before Georgia could reply he had left the room. The imprint of Dominic's lips on her forehead left a burning mark. She scrambled under the blanket and, tucking it firmly around her body, fell instantly asleep.

* * *

A loud banging reverberated in Georgia's ears.

'W . . . what?' She kicked out at the

blanket cocooning her body, unsure at first of her surroundings. A crick in her neck made her wince with pain.

'It's all right. I'll get it,' Dominic shouted from the dining-room.

'Yes, I'm coming,' he called out as Gulliver set up a barking loud enough to wake the dead.

Memories of the previous evening came flooding back as Georgia remembered how she and Dominic had been stranded and taken refuge in the inn with Hilda and how they had been forced to spend the night there. She gulped and hoped it wasn't Belle Jeffreys or Max at the door, then berating herself for being foolish, did some stretches of her own to ease the niggling ache in her back.

The hammering stopped and Georgia heard the low murmur of voices in the corridor.

'It's all right.' Dominic appeared in the doorway a few moments later. Gulliver padded into the room behind him and settled down in front of the embers of the log fire. 'It's the man from the security company. Do you think you could go and see if Hilda's awake? I'll get some coffee on the go.'

Georgia mounted the stairs on legs that were still shaky. 'Hilda?' she called out, 'it's me, Georgia. Are you up?'

She poked her head round Hilda's bedroom door.

'Hello, dear, did you sleep well?' She was sitting at her dressing table brushing her hair. She smiled at Georgia. 'There's hot water if you'd like a shower, help yourself.'

'Thank you.' Georgia ran a hand through her unruly hair. 'Actually the reason I came up is because the man from the security company is downstairs.'

'Goodness, he's very early. I'm so glad you and Dominic slept over. I wouldn't want the poor man to think I wasn't here.'

'Dominic is seeing to him now.'

'I'll be down in a second. Would you get the milk off the doorstep?'

The sun was warm and in the daylight The Highwayman didn't look nearly so threatening as it had the night before. Georgia could see the flowers in the front garden had been neatly tended and the lawn recently mown. She bent down and picked up two cartons of milk. Out of the corner of her eye she caught the flash of a car as it passed by in the road outside. Moments later it reversed back at break neck speed.

'Georgia? It is you, isn't it?' The voice was full of relief.

'Jake?' She shaded her eyes against the morning sun. 'What are you doing here?'

'I've been out looking for you. We thought something dreadful had happened.'

He jumped from the car and running towards her, his arms outstretched, wrapped her in a bear hug. She could feel the furious beating of his heart against hers.

'Everyone's been so worried.'

'I would have phoned but the signal died on my mobile.'

'Never mind all that now. Are you all right?'

'I'm absolutely fine,' she assured him, 'and I'm sorry to have caused so much trouble. How did you know I was missing?'

'The police found the cab abandoned. They contacted the control centre and it was then we realised you weren't in the cottage. Patsy was barking her head off. Ray and Val are looking after her by the way. Anyway Ray said you'd gone out to Stretton Wood and I've been driving round for hours looking for you. Hold on while I radio back to the office to let them know you're safe and to tell the police to call off the search.'

Georgia began to feel seriously guilty. She hadn't realised her disappearance would cause quite such a stir.

'The search?'

'Joyriders have been making trouble locally. Actually somebody reported an attempted break-in here the other night. Anyway, the police are trying to get on top of it. That's why they jumped to it when they realised you hadn't been in the car when it was abandoned.'

Georgia's head now reeled.

'If there's coffee on the go,' Jake looked at the milk carton Georgia was clutching 'mine's white with three sugars. It's cold work driving round the countryside at this hour of the morning. Be with you in a minute.'

Dominic and the security man were seated at a table.

'We were wondering what had happened to the milk,' the security man greeted her.

'You'd better make another mug,' Georgia informed Dominic. 'It seems half the county has been scouring the countryside for us.'

'What?' The scar on Dominic's forehead reddened as he raised his eyebrows.

'It's a long story. I'll tell you later.' Georgia gestured with her eyes towards the security man who was checking his equipment.

'Hello, dears.' Hilda bustled in creating a welcome distraction. 'My, what a lot of people. Help yourself to coffee and toast.'

'Good morning, madam.' The security man stood up. 'I understand you've been having problems with hooligans. It seems they were in the woods last night and that they stole a car. A woman's gone missing. It was on the local radio this morning. The police are out looking for her.'

'Good grief,' Dominic mouthed at Georgia. 'What have we done?'

'If you'll come this way.' Hilda appeared not to have heard all the security man said for which Georgia was grateful. 'I'll show you the system.'

Georgia sat down at the table. 'We've stirred up a hornet's nest, that's what.'

'Where is everybody?' Jake's voice floated down the corridor.

'Kitchen's this way,' Georgia called back.

'Who's that?' Dominic stage whispered.

'Jake Shand and he's looking for us.'

Jake appeared in the doorway.

'Hi,' Dominic greeted him. 'I'm really sorry for all the trouble we caused, but Georgia was in good hands.'

'So I can see.' The tone of Jake's voice was icy.

'Your coffee's all ready.' Georgia picked up the percolator. 'Sugar and milk are on the table.'

'You should be getting back, Georgia.' Jake ignored the mug she nudged towards him. 'The control centre is a madhouse.'

Georgia gulped down the remains of her coffee. 'I'm right with you.'

'Hang on. I'll have a quick word with Hilda then I'll come, too.' Dominic stood up. 'Do I understand it that the police found the car?'

'Yes,' Jake replied.

'I suppose Dominic's mobile wasn't in it?' Georgia asked as he went in search of Hilda.

'I've no idea. I was more interested in finding out what had happened to you than to think about Dominic's personal effects. Ray said he told you not to use number six. What were you thinking of?'

'It was the only cab available and what Ray actually said was that it should be all right as long as I wasn't going too far. Unfortunately it died on me immediately after I telephoned you. I went to tell Dominic what had happened and when we got back to the spot where I'd parked, the cab had disappeared.'

'What an exciting time you seem to have had.' The tone of Jake's voice suggested he didn't entirely believe Georgia's version of events. 'Anyone would think it was an elaborate plan to spend time with Dominic Talbot.'

'That's an outrageous thing to say.'

Dominic strolled back into the kitchen. 'I made your goodbyes to Hilda,' he said. 'Are we ready to go?'

'I'll get my handbag,' Georgia was past caring that she still hadn't had her morning shower and that her hair probably resembled a bird's nest in appearance. All she wanted to do was get out of this nightmare and as far away from Dominic as possible.

'See you in the car and sorry,' he said, kissing her ear. 'I didn't mean to get you into trouble.'

Jake turned round in the doorway in time to see the gesture.

'When you're ready?' He scowled at the pair of them.

They completed the journey back in silence. As soon as Jake drove into the forecourt, Georgia jumped out of the car.

'I have to freshen up,' she said, 'Jake will you drive Dominic to wherever he wants to go?'

'Get one of the other drivers to do it,' Jake replied, slamming the driver's door. 'I'm due at the garage this morning. I only came in because I thought you needed help but it seems I was wrong.'

'What's his problem?' Dominic demanded as he clambered out of the passenger door.

‘He’s a bit territorial,’ Georgia improvised.

Through the windows of the control centre she could see their arrival had created something of a stir amongst those present.

‘Want me to explain things to the authorities for you?’ Dominic nodded towards the patrol car parked in a corner of the forecourt.

‘No need.’ Georgia shook her head. ‘I have a good working relationship with the local police.’

‘Well, give them my apologies for all the hassle we’ve caused.’

‘Don’t forget if you’ve lost your personal effects through my negligence put in an insurance claim.’

‘No worries.’ Dominic smiled. ‘At best I’ve only lost a few pencils and I’m sure my mobile will turn up. See you around.’

No doubt the full story of her night’s escapade would be doing the rounds, probably suitably embellished, Georgia thought ruefully as she headed towards the cottage for a shower after arranging for one of the drivers to take Dominic to the station and promising the police she would call in and make a detailed report of the incident as soon as she had a spare moment.

'Patsy's fine,' Ray reassured her from the control centre. 'My wife will bring her over later.'

'Thanks, Ray.'

'The garage will call to collect the cab later and give it the once over. By the way, we found Mr Talbot's mobile phone. It appears to have slipped under the front seat so it was untouched. One of the drivers gave it back to him. Think that's all, apart from one thing.'

'Yes?'

Georgia looked up from her inspection of the duty log.

'Next time think twice before doing an emergency call out.'

She smiled back at him. 'Will do. I expect New Cabs will make mileage out of it when they find out what happened.'

'They say there's no such thing as bad publicity so I shouldn't worry about it too much, and I think New Cabs probably already know the details.'

'How come?'

'Jake was pretty annoyed and was sounding off in all directions. He wanted the police to call out the helicopter.'

Georgia tried not to dwell on the implications of that one.

'Anything else?'

'Max Doyle rang.'

'Max?' Georgia's voice caught in her throat. 'What did he want?'

'Like everyone else he'd heard about your disappearance. He sounded quite concerned. You'd better call him.'

'Georgia.' Max answered on the second ring. 'Are you OK?'

'I'm fine.'

'Last I heard you'd been abducted or some such nonsense.'

'The story has been exaggerated. Let's leave it at that.'

'If you say so,' Max agreed.

'Thanks for calling.' Georgia made to ring off.

'Are we on for dinner tonight?' Max

asked. 'No strings attached? We could make it a business expense if you insist.'

'I have a lot of work to catch up on.'

'Tomorrow then?'

'I'm not sure,' Georgia replied.

'Don't leave it too long. We need to talk,' Max was saying as Georgia hung up.

The rest of the day passed in a flood of local media interviews and the police pressing for her written account of exactly what had happened regarding the cab. It was late into the evening before Georgia was finished.

Ray's wife had returned Patsy to the cottage when she came to pick her husband up at the end of his shift.

'She's in the conservatory,' Val mouthed through the glass door of Georgia's office.

Engaged on yet another telephone call, Georgia waved her thanks as she carried on speaking. Ray had been right. Her escapade had provided a lot of sales opportunities and whilst Georgia didn't wholly approve of using such methods to gain extra business contacts, she was forced to agree it would be foolish not to turn the situation to her advantage by creating new marketing opportunities.

'I'm off,' she finally called over to the night cover. 'Any problems, I'll be in the cottage.'

Any fears Georgia had that her parents had not heard about the incident were dashed when she later received a garbled telephone call from her mother demanding to know exactly what had happened.

After spending a fraught quarter-of-an-hour calming her down, Georgia was more than ready for a bath. Her muscles still felt stiff from her enforced night's sleep on Hilda's sofa. Putting on her favourite CD she relaxed in a pine-scented steamy haze and let the film music she had chosen soothe her tension away.

Annoyed with herself to realise that every time she closed her eyes an image of Dominic Talbot's rugged features flashed into her mind's eye, she eventually clambered out of the bath and vigorously got dried.

Picking up the remote control she flicked the television on to a news channel and began blow-drying her hair. An image of Belle Jeffreys flashed on to the screen. Standing beside her was Dominic Talbot. The caption underneath read, *Actress Belle Jeffreys and her constant companion Dominic Talbot were tonight en route to the Caribbean.*

'After Dominic's terrible experience,' Belle fluttered her eyelashes at the camera 'I decided he needed to get away from it all and that's exactly what we are going to do.'

'So is the romance between the two of you on again?' the interviewer asked.

'No comment,' Belle simpered with a coy glance up at Dominic who stared impassively at the camera.

Georgia flicked off the news and with determined strokes of the brush that brought tears to her eyes, carried on drying her hair.

A Lodger Arrives

'I can't wait much longer. Have you thought any more about my proposal?'

Georgia took a deep breath as she listened to Max's crackly voice down the telephone line.

'Max, what are you talking about?' she asked as she logged out of her accounts program. Figure work was not one of her strengths and she welcomed any distraction, even if the price she had to pay was talking to Max Doyle.

'What everyone's been talking about for the last month or so. Dod Manor?' he queried with exaggerated patience.

'Oh, that.'

'Yes, that,' Max imitated her disinterested tone of voice.

'Sorry, no, I haven't.'

'Honestly,' Max complained. 'I swear you'd give me better service if I were a twitcher with a crush on a barn owl.'

'Max, I really don't have time for idle chatter.'

'Neither do I. What about that dinner date? You never did come back to me. We could meet up tonight.'

'Tonight?' Georgia echoed faintly.

'I have been remarkably patient and if you think you'll be getting a better offer of a free meal from Dominic Talbot, then I have to tell you he's still holed up in a secret Caribbean hideaway with the beautiful Belle Jeffreys.'

'What Dominic and Belle do in their spare time is of absolutely no interest to me,' Georgia snapped in reply.

'Glad to hear it,' Max replied.

'And I am not in the market for a free meal, either.'

She had heard nothing from Dominic ever since she'd seen the newsflash about his holiday with Belle. Annoyed with herself for having believed his story that there was nothing between them, she decided it was time to get on with her own life and to ensure that the next time Dominic Talbot rang for a driver she would most definitely not be available.

'So, dinner tonight? We can go Dutch if that would ease your conscience.'

'If it's to discuss special rates for your syndicate, then I have to tell you, Max, it's no deal.'

'You drive a hard bargain, Georgia, you know that?'

'That's as may be, but my profit margins have been cut to zero. We offer a good service and I'm not prepared to discount my prices any further.'

'What about if I owned a racehorse?' Max suggested. 'Or took up Chinese silk painting? Would I be in with a chance?'

A reluctant smile curved Georgia's lips. 'Not even then, I'm sorry to say. So did you want to book a cab at full price or is this a social call?'

'Bit of both, really,' Max admitted. 'I am at a loose end this evening and we both have to eat. Sure I can't tempt you to a meal out?'

Georgia looked at the remains of her lunch. The plate was still on her desk together with a half-eaten packet of jelly babies. It had, she realised, been a while since she'd enjoyed a proper meal.

'All right,' she replied.

'Eight o'clock?'

'Fine.'

'There's this new Italian place I've heard quite good reports about. We could give it a try?'

'I'll see you there.'

'You won't stand me up, will you?' he asked.

'I'll try not to,' Georgia replied, enjoying the sensation of being in control. 'Call coming through,' she said as Max began to speak again. 'I have to go.'

'I have Dominic Talbot on the line,' Ray said.

'Could you tell him I'm unavailable?'

'Sure.'

'And no more calls this afternoon.'

'Understood.'

Placing her staff in awkward situations wasn't something Georgia liked to do, but she hadn't actually asked Ray to fib on her behalf. She needed to get the accounts into some sort of reasonable shape before submitting them for audit and for that she needed no interruptions.

A tap on her door drew her attention away from the screen of her laptop.

'Clocking off now,' Ray advised her.

'Goodness, is that the time?' Georgia began tidying her desk.

'Date tonight?' Ray enquired.

'I'm meeting up with someone, yes.'

'Dominic Talbot's been on the line several times. Thought you ought to know. It seems he's back in the country.'

Georgia's heart sank. She had a feeling Dominic wasn't the sort of man to go away without a fight.

Georgia nodded. 'Thanks for dealing with it, Ray. Next time I'll speak to him.' She glanced at her watch again. 'Let's hope he's given up for the day. See you in the morning. By the way, is anyone available to drive me out to the Italian restaurant tonight?'

'We've got several drivers on call. I'll fix one up for you.'

Georgia decided to wear her mint

green trouser suit for dinner with Max. It was smart and, teamed with a brightly coloured silk scarf, casual enough for an evening date. It was an outfit she enjoyed wearing and she knew she looked good in it.

Ensuring Patsy was comfortable in the conservatory she made her way across to the control centre.

'Cab's all ready, Georgia,' the controller informed her, then, lowering his voice, said, 'Ray's asked the new guy to drive you. He thought you'd like to check him out. The driver doesn't actually know who you are so see how you get on with him.'

'Good idea. Thanks.'

'Have a nice evening.'

'Ms Jones?' A smartly dressed man in his mid-twenties approached her in the car park.

'Yes.'

'I'm Sam, your driver for the evening. Where would you like to go?'

They reached The Chianti in reasonable time. Georgia was pleased Sam only made casual conversation during the journey and didn't play loud music in the back of the cab, another of her pet hates.

'There's no need to wait,' she said.

'Here's our card,' Sam said. 'The number is on it if you want to book a cab at the end of your evening.'

'Thank you. Keep the change.' She added a generous tip.

'Would you like me to see you inside?' he asked. 'Sometimes ladies on their own like to be escorted into a restaurant.'

'That's very kind of you,' Georgia began, recognising a good sales service they could offer lone females. Sam was obviously going to be an asset.

'Cab three?' His radio crackled into life.

'Looks like you're in for a busy night.' She smiled. 'Thanks for the offer, but I'll see my way inside. You'd better get that call.'

Max was already waiting for her at one of the small tables on the little balcony that overlooked the gardens.

He stood up and pulled out her chair.

'Is this table all right for you?'

'Fine.' She slid into her seat and a waiter immediately appeared with a menu.

Max ordered two glasses of house white and Georgia put her menu to one side.

'Not hungry?' he asked.

'Lasagne will be fine,' Georgia replied.

'Good choice. I'll have the same.'

They looked at each other for a few moments. Georgia could tell Max had made an effort with his appearance. He was a man who took his personal image seriously. His suits were chosen with care and she saw he was wearing the blue shirt and tie she had given him last Christmas when they had still been together.

'So,' he asked, 'what have you been doing with yourself, apart from staying in haunted inns with Dominic Talbot?'

'That was an unfortunate incident,' she replied, anxious to put the record straight with Max. 'Nothing more, and

I haven't seen Dominic since.'

Like Jake, he might be under the impression she had engineered the whole thing. Ever since the incident Jake had taken pains to stay out of her way. Dominic had flown off to a secret hideaway with Belle and Georgia had thrown herself into her work.

'I couldn't believe it when I caught up with the local news and saw your face staring back at me. It was quite a publicity coup. Didn't know you had it in you.'

'Max.' Georgia hardened her voice. 'It wasn't like that.'

'Course it wasn't,' he said, the tone of his voice suggesting he didn't believe her but that he was prepared to go along with her stance for appearance sake.

'Are there any developments on Dod Manor?' Georgia changed the subject as their lasagne arrived. 'That is what you wanted to talk about?'

'It's a huge project, but, yes, we have the finance in place.' Max paused to swallow some lasagne. 'This is really good, isn't it? Remember we planned to visit Tuscany at some point in the future?'

If there was a subtext to Max's choosing an Italian restaurant for their dinner date, then Georgia steeled herself not to be swayed by his brand of charm. Max was adept at using situations to his advantage and she knew from her own personal experience, he could be ruthless with other people's emotions.

A bleeping noise indicated an incoming call on Max's mobile.

'Sorry,' he apologised. 'I need to take it.'

He moved away from the table. Although Georgia always turned her phone off when she was out socially, she decided to follow Max's example. She saw with dismay she had three missed calls and there were all from Dominic.

Max arrived back at the table at the same time as the waiter delivered the coffee.

'Filming is due to start at Dod Manor at the end of the week,' he explained, 'so it's all systems go. You could be in for a busy time.'

'We've not been approached by anyone,' Georgia replied. 'I expect the film company has its own infrastructure to deal with transport logistics.'

'I could put in a word for you?'

Georgia shook her head. The offer was tempting but she didn't want to be beholden to Max in case he called in the favour.

'Surely you don't want New Cabs to grab all the business?'

'I've been talking to my accountant and our figures are healthy.'

'If you don't expand you'll stand still and anyone knows that's not healthy.'

'Thank you for that piece of business advice, Max. I'll bear it in mind the next time I talk to my father.'

Max blinked. 'How are your parents and the new arrival?' he asked.

'They're fine.'

'Not thinking of staying down there permanently is he?' Max asked carefully. 'Your father?'

Georgia stirred her coffee carefully. She had been right all along to suspect Max of an ulterior motive. Like Abe Shand she suspected he wanted a foot in the door of Georgia Cabs.

'I really have no idea,' she replied. 'We haven't discussed his plans. Thank you for dinner, Max. You really must let me pay.'

The look on his face told Georgia he realised he had gone too far.

'Not at all. It was my invitation. You can pay next time, if you like,' he added with a smile.

'I don't think so.'

Georgia signalled to the waiter and placed her credit card on the bill.

'We're both going to be extremely busy in the coming months.'

She stood up.

'You must let me see you home.' Max pushed back his chair.

'I have a driver waiting for me,' she replied.

There was no need to cross her fingers. Sam had told her he was available all evening.

Not bothering to see if Max was following her, Georgia headed for the door. She stood on the pavement outside, debating the best course of action to take, before realising a cab was slowly edging towards her.

'Sam?' She recognised him with a smile as he wound down the driver's window. 'It's good to see you. You haven't been waiting all evening, have you?'

'No, Madam. I had a fare and he asked me to wait outside the restaurant until you came out.'

'What?' she asked in confusion.

It was then she realised the shadow in the rear of the car was a passenger. He leaned forward.

'Georgia, we have to speak and if I have to sit here all night waiting for you to finish your date with Max Doyle then I will.'

It was Dominic Talbot.

* * *

'Problem?' Max hovered at Georgia's elbow. 'Hi, there. Dominic, isn't it?' He leaned forward and peered into the cab. 'Didn't see you hiding away in the back. Paparazzi on your tail again?'

Dominic greeted him with a terse, 'Max,' ignoring his feeble attempt at a joke.

'So,' Max said after a moment's silence. 'What are you doing here? If you've come to offer Georgia a lift — ' he began to say.

'He has and I've accepted,' Georgia butted in, yanking the passenger door open so suddenly Dominic almost fell out on to the pavement.

'Steady on,' he remonstrated, rubbing his shoulder.

'Bye, Max. Nice seeing you.'

Georgia jumped into the car, half landing on Dominic, who was doing his best to sort himself out on the back seat. Her eyes met those of Sam in the driver's mirror.

'Need any help, madam?' he asked.

'I'm fine, thank you. I, er, hope I can rely on your tact and discretion about all this?'

'Goes without saying,' he replied cheerfully, suggesting Georgia's cover had been blown. She suspected Sam was now well aware that he had his boss in the back of his cab.

'Take us back to Dod Cottage, will you, please?' she asked.

Sam eased the car away from the kerb, leaving Max gaping after them.

'I'll give you a call,' he mouthed, beginning to trot along the pavement as Sam increased his speed.

'I've been trying to contact you,' Dominic complained as soon as Georgia was settled.

'I wasn't taking calls.'

'You talked to Max,' he pointed out.

Georgia took a deep breath but before she could speak Dominic said, 'All this is besides the point. What I wanted to talk to you about was . . . '

Georgia shook her head, gesturing to the back of Sam's head with her eyes. There was no partition between the driver and his passengers and she didn't want Sam overhearing whatever it was

Dominic wanted to get off his chest.

She turned her head away from him and watched the fading light deepen the hedgerow to dark purple as the countryside flashed past them.

Sam was a careful driver but Georgia could not relax. She was all the time aware of Dominic's presence beside her. It was all Georgia could do not to let out a sigh of relief as Sam turned into the airfield entrance to the cab compound and came to a halt in front of Dod Cottage.

'Thank you, Mr Talbot,' Sam said, adding for Georgia's benefit, 'the fare's been settled by the gentleman, madam.'

'Well done, Sam,' Dominic patted him on the shoulder. 'You did a great job.'

'You'd better come inside,' Georgia spoke to Dominic. 'Can you be available to drive Mr Talbot home?' she asked Sam.

'I'll go and get a cup of tea in the office. Ring through when you're ready, sir,' he said to Dominic.

'Very neatly handled,' he murmured in her ear as Georgia unlocked the door to her flat.

'You do realise my reputation will be in tatters if you carry on like this?'

Dominic looked suitably chastened.

'Sorry,' he mumbled, then added with a twinkle of his blue eyes, 'that colour green suits you. Pity you wore it for Max's benefit. Are you two back together again?' he enquired innocently.

'I have to take Patsy out.' Georgia went through the connecting door to the conservatory.

'I'll come with you,' Dominic said. 'I could do with some fresh air and exercise after being cramped in that cab all evening.'

'I object to you spying on me.' Georgia's raised voice set Patsy barking.

'How else was I going to speak to you?' Dominic demanded. 'You don't answer my calls and I've got repetitive strain injury from texting you. Look.'

He held up his hands. The sleeves of his casual top were pushed back to reveal sun tanned forearms. The hairs on his arms looked so springy Georgia experienced an annoying urge to stroke them to see if they were as soft as they looked. He peered at her through his fingers.

'You don't look at all concerned,' he complained.

Georgia unlocked the door to the conservatory. 'That's because I don't believe you,' she replied, shooing Patsy outside. 'Don't be long,' she called after her.

'I don't blame you for feeling cross,' he began. 'Can I explain?'

Outside she could hear Patsy snuffling in the grass. Georgia welcomed the cool night breeze, fanning her cheeks and hoped her colour wasn't too heightened.

'That's enough,' she called after Patsy. 'Come on in.'

The little bell on her collar jangled as she trotted back towards them. To Georgia's annoyance she made straight for Dominic and sniffed the hem of his trousers.

'I've been traipsing round muddy fields most of the day,' he explained. 'I expect I'm covered in all sorts of exciting organic wild life,' he said, patting Patsy's head. 'Er, are we going to have words down here or shall we go through to your flat?'

'Go through, please.' Georgia, doing her best to inject some dignity into the situation, indicated the stairs.

Her small kitchenette seemed to shrink in Dominic's presence. He leaned against a worktop as she filled a kettle.

'I can offer you some tea. Coffee keeps me awake if I drink it this late at night.'

'Whatever.' Dominic smiled. 'Belle Jeffreys . . . ' he began.

'Can you get the milk out of the fridge?' Georgia asked.

Dominic bent down and did as he was told.

'You can fiddle around with that kettle for ever but eventually you are going to have to listen to me,' he said, 'because I don't intend leaving until you do.'

Realising Dominic had her over a barrel, Georgia filled the two mugs with tea and sat down at the table.

'I can guess what you must have thought when you learned about Belle and me going away together,' he began.

'It really doesn't matter.'

'It does,' Dominic insisted. 'I told you there was nothing between us.'

'And I believed you, which only goes to prove I was a fool. It's a mistake I shan't make again.'

'No, you weren't, and you didn't make a mistake.' Dominic ran a hand through his scrubby chestnut hair making it stand on end. 'Against my wishes Belle has been cast as the lead in this production. I feel she is totally wrong for the part. Katherine, the young heroine, is a shy, pale-skinned brunette who blushes every time a man speaks to her. She is not a confident blonde I voiced my opinion to the director but he didn't see things my way. He says she's box office and her physical attributes are nothing a good make-up department can't fix.'

'I expect that's so.'

Dominic waved away Georgia's interruption.

'That's why it was arranged for us to go away together to bond as the director put it. He'd been trying to get in touch with me that night we were stranded. I didn't know anything about it in advance. Let me tell you, one day spent in the close confines of a Caribbean beach cabin with Belle is more than enough. She has two topics of conversation. When she's finished telling you all about herself she then asks you what you think of her career prospects. That girl came dangerously close to being chucked into the pool on more than one occasion.'

'Forgive me if I don't feel sorry for you,' Georgia said. 'They do have telephones in paradise, don't they, these days, not to mention internet connections?'

Dominic drank some of his tea. 'I wanted to tell you to your face. Besides the signal was down for a lot of the time, due to high winds or something. You don't have a biscuit by any chance, do you? I missed dinner.'

'Whose fault is that?'

'Mine,' Dominic admitted with a shame-faced smile.

'Haven't you eaten anything?' Georgia refused to be taken in by his look of penitence.

'I shared half a bar of chocolate with Sam.'

'Here.' Georgia produced a tin of flapjacks. 'Ray's wife made them.'

'I think I'm going to enjoy working in deepest Fenland, if this is an example of the local cuisine.' He waved an oaty wedge of dried apricot and honey at her. 'Exotic fruit is all very well but it's not very filling, is it? After a while pineapples start to pall.'

'Where's Belle now?'

'She's staying at The Duck. Half the unit is. We're all madly trying to find accommodation away from each other. You've no idea how easy it is to get on someone's nerves when you're cooped up together. At the end of a shoot you can bet half the cast won't be speaking to the other half and the ones who have survived the experience often want to throttle each other.'

'All this is very interesting.' Georgia nibbled absently on a flapjack as Dominic wolfed down a third. 'But I still don't see what it has to do with me.'

'I want you to be my personal driver and I needed to get my request in first.'

'What?' Georgia's hand clipped the edge of her mug, spilling tea all over the table.

'New Cabs aren't proving as reliable as we thought they were going to be.' Dominic began to calmly wipe up the mess. 'People are being left stranded all over the place. You will do it, won't you? Be my personal driver?'

'No.' Georgia shook her head.

'Why not?'

'I have other demands on my time.'

'You have a laptop, don't you?'

'Of course.'

'Then bring it along with you. There's always loads of hanging around on a shoot. You can catch up between takes. People bring all sorts of things with them to while away the time; books, needlework, crosswords.'

'Why do you need a driver all to yourself? Surely you can muck in with everybody else?'

'Rewrites,' Dominic replied through a mouthful of flapjack.

'You have a laptop, too, don't you? Doesn't your advice to me hold? You can rewrite on the set.'

'I need to get the feel of a place. The director's got it in his head to do some of the indoor shoots at another property a few miles away. I have to dash about all over the place and I never did finish my research in the woods.' He paused. 'And I'd like to revisit The Highwayman.'

'What on earth for?'

'According to the storyline the heroine has a liaison with an unsuitable man and I rather thought it would be a good place.'

'It's falling down and the new people might not agree.'

'You'd be amazed what can be done with a bit of clever lighting and some imaginative back drops, and I'm sure the new people could do with some extra cash.'

'Look, if you need a driver, I'm sure Sam would be more than willing to work for you.'

'I don't want Sam,' Dominic said with a mulish jut of his jaw. 'I want you.'

'For goodness' sake, why?'

'Belle suspects there's something between us.'

'In that case I definitely do not want to get involved. I've enough baggage in my personal life without adding to it. I'll call her in the morning and put her right.'

'No, you don't understand. I don't want her put right.'

'Why ever not?'

'I don't want to get involved with Belle Jeffreys.'

'If you think you can use me as a means to sort out your tangled love life then you've got another thing coming.' Georgia's chair leg scraped the floor as she stood up. 'Now, if you've finished emptying my flapjack tin I think you'd better give Sam a quick call.'

'Is that all you can say?' Dominic asked, leisurely shrugging on his leather jacket.

'Without losing my dignity, yes.'

'Do you know when you're annoyed you get two bright red spots of colour on your cheekbones?' Dominic grinned. 'I rather like it.'

Georgia tossed back her head. 'The door is there,' she said pointedly.

'I can take a hint. I'll be in touch. Take care.'

* * *

'Jake Shand said he can't cover,' Ray informed Georgia who was busy trying to make sense of the depleted duty roster.

'Is he sick?'

'He didn't say. That's the fifth today. I've never known anything like it.' He coughed then sneezed into a tissue.

'You're not going down with anything, are you?' Georgia looked up with an anxious frown.

'Hope not.'

'Keep drinking lots of water.' Georgia pointed to the bottle of mineral water on his desk. 'I'm relying on you. Please don't let me down.'

'Have I ever?' Ray asked with the suspicion of a croak in his voice. 'By the way,' he flapped a piece of paper at her 'the film unit manager wants to know if we have any rooms available.'

'Sorry?'

'Seems The Duck can't accommodate everyone so they're ringing round to see if there are any alternatives.'

'Surely they're not reduced to putting people up in cabs for the night?'

'Hardly, but they wondered if anyone had a spare room they'd be prepared to rent out. You've got one, haven't you?'

'Ray, where is this leading?' Georgia demanded.

'We've got to do our bit for the community, isn't that what you're always telling us?'

'Yes,' Georgia admitted reluctantly.

'Like it or not we do need to get involved in this filming project. Abe Shand has outbid us on every front so far. We are losing out on bookings.'

'I'd heard his reputation wasn't living up to his publicity.'

'He's still in business and it doesn't do to underestimate the opposition.'

'You've got a point, I suppose,' Georgia agreed.

'What better opportunity is there than to have someone from the unit in house? They'll be bound to put in a good word for us.'

'There is the spare room at the back of my flat. I'd be prepared to offer it to a temporary lodger, but make sure they don't send a man,' she told Ray.

Although she hadn't heard from Dominic since the night of her date with Max, Georgia didn't want him learning of her accommodation availability and getting ideas of rooming at Dod Cottage.

Later Ray said to her, 'I passed your details on to one of the film unit managers. She seemed very grateful about the offer of a spare room and said to say thanks. She was going to put the word round immediately.'

The sound of a car outside drew Georgia's attention to the window. She frowned.

'Oh, no,' she muttered under her breath as she spied Belle Jeffreys sitting in the back seat, regally waiting for the driver to open the passenger door. 'What's she doing here?'

'Can I help you?' Georgia went outside then watched in amazement as the driver began to unload cases from the boot. 'Er, what are you doing?' she asked.

'I've come to stay,' Belle announced. 'Put the bags over there,' she instructed the driver, pointing to the cottage.

'I beg your pardon?'

Belle turned back to Georgia with an expression on her face that indicated she was being more than a nuisance.

'Your face is familiar.'

'I'm Georgia Jones and I live here.'

'So you're my new landlord?' Belle looked her up and down, her deep violet eyes appraising her appearance. 'You're Dominic's friend, aren't you?'

'I'm your what?' Georgia wasn't sure she had heard Belle correctly.

'We'll sort out the details later.' Belle turned her attention back to the cottage. 'Right now I need to have a good soak in a hot tub. I take it you do have running water in this neck of woods? I mean, I love period architecture and all that, but facilities can get a bit basic at times. Like it or not, I'm your new lodger. What better way to keep an eye on you and Dominic?'

'No.' Georgia blinked in horror as Belle teetered towards the cottage on impossibly high heels.

'Need any help?'

Belle's expression changed instantly at the sound of a male voice calling up the stairs.

'Yes, please,' she gushed. 'I don't know who you are but we could do with a big strong man.'

'Max Doyle. I'll deal with your luggage.'

After a bit more confusion on the staircase, Max struggled to the top with Belle's luggage.

'There, all in.'

'You are an angel. Thank you so much.' She gave a light laugh. 'I'm Belle Jeffreys,' she introduced herself.

'I know who you are and I'm very pleased to meet you,' Max said with his charming smile, 'and may I say I am a fan?'

'No, really? I'm surprised you recognised me. So many people don't. I quite often forget I'm famous.'

Georgia watched Belle flutter her false eyelashes at Max in a gesture of faux modesty.

'And may I also add that the small

screen doesn't do you justice?'

'Don't let anyone hear you say that.' Belle was getting into her stride. Georgia suspected this was the sort of conversation she liked. 'At the moment the small screen is my medium. It doesn't do to knock it, although I agree television work can be restricting.'

'If it's not a rude question,' Max asked, 'what are you doing here?'

'This lady . . . ' Belle turned to Georgia. 'I'm so sorry, but I've completely forgotten your name.'

'Hi, Georgia,' said Max, grinning at her. 'I didn't know you and Belle were friends.'

'We're not,' Belle was quick to put in. 'Georgia offered me the use of one of her rooms and, after a little persuasion, I accepted.'

Georgia gaped. She couldn't fault Belle for ingenuity.

'So you'll be staying here?'

'Yes.'

'In that case I expect we'll be seeing a lot more of each other.'

'Is this a social call?' Georgia butted in.

'I only wanted to make sure you got home safely after Dominic picked you up outside the restaurant.'

'When was this?' Belle demanded, looking from Max to Georgia. She was no longer smiling.

'Georgia and I had dinner at The Chianti. At the end of the evening we discovered Dominic lurking around outside looking decidedly shifty.'

'Thank you for your concern, Max,' Georgia replied as Belle scribbled something on the back of an envelope and passed it over to Max.

'Can I give you a lift anywhere, Ms Jeffreys?' Max asked Belle.

'Please, call me Belle,' she insisted. 'Actually there are still one or two of my things at The Duck, if it's not too inconvenient. I said I would have them moved as soon as possible.'

'Consider it done.'

Suspicion Falls On Jake

Georgia felt the beginnings of a headache pounding her forehead as she walked over to the office from Dod Cottage. She rubbed a hand across her brow. As she had feared, Belle was proving to be a demanding lodger.

'The hot water is tepid,' she complained after having drained the system with her rigorous bathing and hair-washing routine and rinsing out goodness knows how many delicate articles of clothing.

'I'm sure The Duck can better accommodate your needs.' Georgia tried yet again to move Belle on.

As usual when Belle was on a roll she didn't listen to anyone's voice but her own. 'Also, can someone valet my room? There are clothes all over the floor.'

'That's because you dropped them there. I suggest you pick them up,' Georgia replied. 'Because if you don't, no one else will. I would also suggest you dust the room and keep it clean.'

After their full and frank exchange of views Belle made a token attempt to keep her room reasonably tidy, but she still continued to grumble.

Max, too, had taken to dropping in at a moment's notice and most evenings he and Belle would sit together on the sofa, talking and drinking wine, until, forced by fatigue, Georgia would crawl up to bed. She didn't care if Max had a thing going with Belle or was trying to make her jealous, she needed her beauty sleep.

'Have you heard the news?' Ray greeted Georgia as she walked into the office the next day.

'What now?' she asked with a sigh.

'It's Abe Shand on the line.' Ray put a hand over the receiver. 'Don't agree to anything until we've had a word,' he stage whispered.

Intrigued, Georgia took the call in the office.

'Georgia? Hi, there.'

'Abe,' she replied. 'What can I do for you?'

'Since that son of mine seems to be dragging his heels, I wondered if you'd given any more thought to the merger?'

'What merger?' Georgia demanded.

'He didn't mention it to you?'

'I haven't seen Jake for a while,' Georgia replied.

'I suppose you think you've been clever making up to Dominic Talbot?' There was the suggestion of a sneer in his voice. 'Poor old Jake didn't stand a chance, did he? Is that why you're not so close to my boy these days?'

'Abe, what are you talking about?'

'Since Jake won't put it on the line, I will. It's time to get down to business. I'm talking about a proposed merger of New Cabs and Georgia Cabs.'

'Abe, this really is not an appropriate time.'

'I think it is.'

'Because my father's in Australia?' Georgia bit back at him.

She could tell by the silence down

the line that her suspicions were correct.

'I assume you have his full authority to act?' he asked.

'This conversation stops right here and now,' Georgia said firmly. 'Was there anything else?'

'You may come to regret your hasty decision,' Abe replied.

'I don't think so. Now, if you'll excuse me, I have an extremely busy morning.'

She cut the call and took a few moments out to compose herself before going back into the outer office.

'So, New Cabs?' she asked, 'what's the latest?'

'Was Abe trying to broker a deal?' Ray asked.

'Something along those lines.'

'I'll say this for the man, he's certainly got a nerve.'

'What's happened?' Georgia demanded.

'New Cabs have over extended themselves by undercutting us and their profit margins have slumped. They are in serious financial difficulties.'

'Is this official or only cab-room gossip?

'I heard it from one of their drivers. I think that's why we haven't seen much of Jake recently. He's probably too embarrassed to show his face around here.'

'This is nothing to do with Jake.'

'That's something else I've been trying to tell you. His father was using him to infiltrate our operation.'

'That's nonsense.'

'Is it?' Ray raised an eyebrow. 'He started all that mix-up over the brief-cases. Terry can't be sure, but he thinks Jake hid Dominic's under the filing cabi-net on purpose. Then when I checked our log, it was Jake who filled cab six with dirty petrol.'

'That could be nothing more than a coincidence.'

'That's why he panicked and came looking for you when he thought you'd been abducted in the woods. I think he was scared that after cab six let you down, you'd start putting two and two together and look more deeply into the issues between our two companies. I've been checking some of the drives he did for us and it seems he was handing out New Cabs business cards as well as our own.'

Georgia felt a sharp pain in her chest as she blinked at Ray.

'Are you sure?'

Ray nodded. 'Sorry, Georgia.'

'Where is Jake now? Do you have any idea?'

'According to his garage he's on two weeks' leave.'

Georgia shook her head, still unable to believe what Ray was telling her.

Monday mornings always passed in a blur of activity. Early summer weekends were some of their busiest times. The arts centre students needed transport back to the station after their courses and there had been an overnight corporate affair at the stud, necessitating a shuttle service of taxis to and from the station.

'I've never known anything like it,' Ray said as he finally managed to make them some coffee about two in the afternoon. 'I think word has got round about New Cabs and people are wary of calling them. It's been non-stop.'

'Thanks.' Georgia accepted a biscuit and drank some of the coffee. 'If things go on like this then we'll need some of the New Cabs drivers.'

'Several of them have been calling in, too. I've got a list of available drivers.'

'Nothing from the film set?' Georgia tried to keep the question casual.

'No, but I'm still of the opinion Georgia Cabs were the victims of a stitch-up job by Jake and his father. Abe's desperate for business and he's not above fighting dirty.'

'Jake's not like that, though, is he?'

'His pride took a bit of a blow after that business with Dominic at The Highwayman.'

'Why does that episode keep coming back to haunt me?' Georgia ran a hand through her hair.

Ray glanced at his watch. 'Time for the school run, I think.'

'Need any help?'

'We're fine.'

'In that case I'm just popping back to the cottage. Patsy needs to be let out.'

Georgia breathed in the cool smell of recent rain. There had been an earlier shower and the grass was damp under her feet.

Slipping through the conservatory side door she called out for Patsy.

'Where are you? Fancy a quick walk?'

There was no patter of feet on the tiles.

'Patsy?' Georgia called out again. 'Are you there?'

She mounted the stairs, hoping she hadn't found her way into Belle's bedroom.

She heard a yelp of recognition behind her and spun round.

'There you are. What have you been up to?'

Patsy began jumping up and down outside Belle's door.

'You know you mustn't go in there.'

She tried to drag the dog away. As her fingers curled round Patsy's collar she heard a faint groan coming from inside the room.

'Belle?' Georgia tapped on the door. 'Are you in there? Is everything all right? Belle?' She raised her voice when there was no reply. 'Can I come in?'

Trying to push open the door, she met an obstacle. Further inspection revealed it to be a pair of feet. Peering round the gap she stared in amazement at the sight that met her eyes.

Max was prone on the floor, his feet entangled in something that looked suspiciously like an item of Belle's clothing and he was nursing an egg-sized bump on his forehead.

'Am I interrupting something?'

Georgia jumped at the sound of a voice behind her. She had been bending over Max's prostrate form. He was clinging on to her hand, a glazed look in his eyes.

'Dominic.' She gasped up at him.

'How did you get in?'

'You left the conservatory door open. What a lot of petals.'

The floor was strewn with the remains of a bouquet of white roses. Max groaned. Georgia tried to get him to relinquish his hold of her hand but Max clung on, his fingers digging into the soft flesh of her palm.

'Patsy, will you get out of the way?' Georgia pushed the dog's wiry body to one side as she attempted to lick Max's fingers.

Dominic stooped down and picked her up.

'Allow me. Is this your doing?' he asked the little dog.

Patsy wriggled excitedly and nuzzled the stubble on Dominic's cheek.

'Are you all right?' Georgia demanded, gently shaking Max's shoulder with her free hand, hoping he wasn't suffering from concussion. 'What happened?'

'I tripped.'

'Does it hurt anywhere?'

'My leg.'

'Can you stand up?'

'I expect he can.' Dominic leaned over Georgia's shoulder, displaying scant sympathy for Max's distress. 'How many fingers?' He held up a hand.

'Please, Dominic, don't interrupt.'

'All he's done is bang his head.'

'There's such a thing as delayed concussion.'

'Being a gentleman,' Dominic was now so close Georgia could feel his breath on the back of her neck. He lowered his voice 'I won't mention that he appears to have been in a lady's bedroom at the time.'

'What I am doing here is none of your business, Talbot,' Max replied, rousing himself as the colour began to return to his cheeks. 'I can assure you, it's all respectable.'

'Sorry.' Dominic made a placatory gesture. 'But the facts speak for themselves, Max.'

'They are also none of your business, so butt out.'

'There.' Dominic looked pleased with himself as he smiled at Georgia. 'He's feeling better already.'

'I've had a nasty bang on the head.' Max moaned.

Georgia knew from experience Max wasn't above milking a situation to his advantage.

'Perhaps you ought to do it yourself,' she suggested. 'See if anything's broken. Where is Belle, by the way?'

'I've no idea,' Max replied.

'Shouldn't she be on set with you?' Georgia asked Dominic.

'Don't glare at me, Georgia.' He smiled down at her. 'I'm not the one lurking around your cottage uninvited.'

'I don't know what either of you is doing here.'

Georgia stood up as Max struggled to a sitting position. 'I certainly didn't invite you in, Dominic, and I would appreciate some form of explanation from you, Max, as well.'

Dominic leaned casually against the door frame. 'You go first, Max.'

'Not now,' he blustered.

'I think out of courtesy you do owe Miss Jones an explanation.' There was no trace of amusement in Dominic's voice now.

'So do you,' Max snapped back.

'You know, I'm beginning to wonder if you might have broken in, since you seem so reluctant to divulge your reason for being here.'

'I didn't break in. Belle lent me her key,' Max mumbled.

'She had no right to do that,' Georgia protested.

'I collected the last of her things from The Duck. The landlord was getting a bit unpleasant about storage and threatening to take Belle's stuff to a charity shop.'

'And we couldn't have that, could we?' Dominic butted in. 'Can you imagine the good wives of Dod Stretton going round the village in Belle's cast offs?' He grinned at Georgia. 'Doesn't bear thinking about.'

'Sorry, Georgia,' Max apologised.

'Perhaps it was unethical of me letting myself in without telling you, but you don't like being disturbed at work and you know you can trust me. After all, I am an old friend.' He cast a glance at Dominic. 'Unlike some. I don't believe you've provided us with an explanation as to why you're here.'

'That's simple. I called into the control centre first for business reasons. Ray told me Georgia was in the cottage. He thought she wouldn't mind my calling in.'

'Why did you want to see me?' Georgia asked.

'I've come to offer you a personal driving commission. There, a perfectly innocent reason for my presence here. Now it's your turn, Max. What are you doing here?'

'If you must know, I was leaving a note for Belle.'

'Is this it?' Dominic pounced on a sheet of pink notepaper buried among the rose petals seconds before Patsy descended on it.

'Give it back to me.'

'Don't tell me you're writing love letters to our leading lady.'

'My relationship with Miss Jeffreys is none of your affair.' Max snatched at the note.

'It is mine when you sneak uninvited into my cottage.' Georgia pursed her lips.

Max finally managed to struggle to his feet and began to brush down his jacket. 'I wanted to invite Belle out to dinner. She has a proposal she wants to discuss with me.'

'Do you normally offer your business companions a bouquet of white roses?' Dominic enquired.

'I thought it would be a nice gesture. A sort of house-warming present.'

Moments later Max was gone. Patsy raced down the stairs after him, leaving Dominic and Georgia facing each other in the cramped confines of Belle's room. Georgia noticed Dominic was having difficulty standing up straight under the beams.

‘Lucky you came back when you did, isn’t it? Goodness knows how long Max would have lain there if you hadn’t found him.’

‘I came back to take Patsy out for a brief walk.’

Georgia didn’t know why she was explaining things to Dominic. She didn’t have to, but it helped to have something neutral to say.

‘I think,’ Georgia did her best to keep her voice steady and to inject some dignity into the situation ‘Belle’s bedroom is not the place to continue our discussion.’

A smile softened Dominic’s mouth. ‘Perhaps you’re right.’ He picked up what was left of Max’s discarded bouquet. ‘What do you suggest we do with these? They look rather sad, don’t they? But I believe a white rose is the flower of peace.’ He thrust them at Georgia. ‘Why don’t you keep them as a peace offering?’

‘They belong to Belle. My favourite flowers are pink carnations and I think you'll find lilies are the flowers of peace.'

'I'll bear all that in mind next time I visit a florists' shop.' Dominic scooped up the petals.

Georgia seized the opportunity to ease past him and slip out of the room.

'There, all done.' Dominic disposed of what remained of the flowers in the kitchen pedal bin and dried his hands on some kitchen paper.

'Are we going for a walk?' he enquired.

Recognising the magic word, Patsy began to bark enthusiastically.

'This way.' Georgia opened the back door that led to the greensward at the rear of the cottage.

'Away from prying eyes, good idea.' Dominic ambled along beside her. 'Actually,' he cleared his throat 'I exaggerated,' he confessed.

'About what?' Georgia picked up a fallen branch and threw it towards the trees. Patsy raced after it.

'My driving commission. It's not

really an emergency,' he explained.

'Then why fib about it?'

'I need someone with local knowledge. Abe Shand says he can supply me with a driver, but his service is getting more unreliable and after that business when he left me stranded at the station, I've got little confidence in his set up.'

'I don't know that we'll be able to meet your needs, either,' Georgia replied.

'Before you turn me down flat, perhaps you should know Abe Shand also said Georgia Cabs weren't interested in taking on any site work.'

'What?' Georgia stumbled on a tuft of grass. Dominic put out a hand to steady her.

'That's what I thought.' Dominic squeezed her elbow as he made a wry face. 'I told the director I would check it out with you to see if it was true.'

'You know it isn't.'

'In that case, to prove Abe is wrong, tomorrow morning? Eight-thirty if that's not too early for you? You can use the booking as an opportunity to put people right on the, er, misunderstanding regarding the availability of Georgia Cabs.'

Georgia hesitated. Was Dominic telling the truth or was it a clever ploy to get his own way? His explanation was perfectly plausible, if it were true.

'You don't look too pleased at the prospect of spending time in my company,' he complained. 'The film unit budget could run to a bit extra so I'm not about to beat you down on price.'

'I'll pick you up at eight-thirty,' she said before she had time to regret her decision.

'No need. I'll get a lift over here from The Duck with one of the crew. Things there improved after Belle moved out. We're all actually speaking to each other again. By the way, thanks for taking her on. You're doing the unit a great service and everyone is in your debt.'

Georgia glanced at her watch. 'I have to get back. If I'm to spend the whole day out tomorrow then I'll need to sort things out in the control room.'

'I thought I mentioned the booking wasn't for a day,' Dominic replied.

'Patsy, come on,' she called out. 'Time to go back.'

'Did you hear what I said?' Dominic raised his voice to drown out Patsy's excited barks.

'What was that?'

'The booking. It's not for a day.'

'How long is it for?' Georgia asked, carefully clipping the lead on to Patsy's collar.

'I'll want your exclusive services for the whole week.'

* * *

'Don't worry,' Dominic reassured Georgia, raising his voice against the constant hum of a generator. 'Things aren't as chaotic as they look. People really do know what they are doing.'

The air was ringing with the sound of enthusiastic hammering. Vehicles revved up in the background, and everyone seemed to be shouting to each other at the top of their voices. Elegantly dressed actors drifted about, delicately stepping over industrial strength cables.

A passing gardener spoke as he trundled up to them pushing a wheelbarrow. 'Where do you want these bedding plants to go, Dominic? I've been told to ask you.'

'Somewhere on the front lawn. I want Katherine to wander through the gardens on her arrival. She'll be wearing a white dress so the scene needs a splash of colour to set the mood.'

Dominic consulted a page of script in front of him. Georgia was doing her best to keep her emotions under control. How she had been talked into accepting a week's commission she didn't know, but as soon as she could think of a way to wriggle out of it, she would leap at the opportunity. For the moment all she could do was put a brave face on things.

'Does everything look right to you?' Dominic asked. 'I'd value a bit of local input. Have we made any glaring-errors?'

'I've never seen Dod Manor look so well tended,' Georgia replied, absorbing the scene in front of her. 'I wouldn't have believed it was possible to transform a wilderness into something resembling an authentic English country garden in such a short space of time.'

'It wasn't easy, but Max's business colleagues were surprisingly helpful. As one or two of them are looking for a quick return on their investment they supplied us with a list of useful contacts and they came up trumps.'

'Max isn't here, is he?' Georgia asked, reluctant to bump into him after the previous day's encounter.

'Not that I know of.' Dominic was still frowning over his rewrite.

'Talking of Max, where's Belle?' Georgia enquired. She was equally as reluctant to bump into the leading actress.

'Probably in her caravan cramming up on the script rewrite I dumped on her last night.' Dominic smiled. 'You don't want her, do you? I'd rather she wasn't disturbed. She's one of the slowest learners of lines in the world and the slightest distraction tips her over the edge.'

Georgia shook her head. 'Things are quite calm at the cottage at the moment and I'd like to keep it that way.'

'You know, Max doesn't strike me as the sort of man to get star struck, but why else would he buying flowers for Belle?' Dominic asked.

'He likes professional, successful women.'

The moment Georgia spoke, she regretted her words.

'Was that why you and he became engaged?' Dominic asked the inevitable question.

'We weren't right for each other.' It no longer hurt Georgia to admit she had made a mistake. 'Can we talk about something else?'

'Of course. Sorry,' Dominic apologised. 'It is none of my business and I shouldn't be standing here gossiping.'

Georgia crossed her arms over her

chest. 'I'm not used to standing around gossiping, either. Isn't there something I can do?'

'You don't fancy being an extra, I suppose?'

'No, I do not,' Georgia objected.

'Pity.' A rueful smile hovered over his lips. 'I rather fancy tying bonnet ribbons under your chin.'

A loud shriek rent the air.

'Now what?' Dominic raised his eyebrows.

'Sam?' Georgia recognised the figure in tight breeches racing towards them. 'What are you doing here?'

'I've been recruited as an extra for the garden party scene.'

'What's all the noise about?' Dominic demanded.

'One of the girls has been splashed by chip-pan fat from the catering van.'

'Does she need A&E?'

'I could drive her over,' Georgia suggested.

'Think she's playing the drama queen,' Sam replied. 'It's only a minor burn, but there was a bit of a fire and things got out of control for a while. It's all back on track now. There's a first-aid box in the cab, isn't there, Georgia? Anything for burns?'

'We have some antiseptic cream.'

'Where's the site nurse?' Dominic butted in. 'She should be seeing to all this.'

'Attending to Belle.'

'She wasn't burnt, too, was she?'

'She's been bitten by something and refusing to come out of her caravan until it's seen to.'

'For goodness' sake,' Dominic protested. 'We are way behind schedule. If we don't start filming soon, the day will be wasted.'

'I've been on a first-aid course,' Georgia volunteered.

'Can you deal with a burn?'

'If it's not too serious.'

'It isn't,' Sam assured her.

'You've got the job,' Dominic called after Georgia, who was already running towards her cab.

Sam pounded along beside her.

'Exciting, isn't it?'

'That's one way of putting it.'

The cab was parked in one of the far fields and by the time they reached it they were both panting.

Sam leant against the side, trying to catch his breath as Georgia rummaged around for the first-aid kit.

'Here.' She thrust the green medical box at him.

'I hope you don't mind me working here as an extra,' Sam said, a concerned look on his face. 'I mean, I love cab driving and that's my proper job, but when they advertised for extras I thought it might be a bit of fun.'

'We'll talk about it later.' Georgia was careful to remove the cab keys after she locked the door.

'I could put the word round about Georgia Cabs, too,' Sam added. 'You know, get us some extra business?'

'Fine with me,' Georgia agreed, 'as long as you don't bad mouth New Cabs or behave unprofessionally.'

The burn did prove to be a mild one

but Georgia insisted the nurse take a proper look after she had initially tended to it. She lost sight of Dominic in the melee of people ambling around and, while she was repacking her first-aid kit, Belle accosted her.

'Look.' She pointed to a puncture mark on her neck. 'I've been bitten.'

'It's not a very big bite,' Georgia said. 'In fact, I can hardly see it.'

'You don't think it's anything to do with Patsy?'

'My Patsy?'

'She's always running around in the grass. Has she picked anything up?'

'She has not,' Georgia retaliated.

'I have very sensitive skin. I can't afford to appear in public covered in flea bites.'

'Patsy does not have fleas.'

'There you are.' One of the crew grabbed Belle by the arm. 'The director has been looking for you everywhere. I hope you're word perfect on the rewrite because he is in no mood for further delays.'

'That girl is impossible,' she said to Sam who was still hovering by her side. 'Do you know she wants the extras to stand in position even when she's not on the set? It's ridiculous. We're all getting windblown and one or two people are suffering from hay fever. They're sneezing all over the place. Something else that's sending Belle into meltdown.'

Dominic trudged up to them. 'They're calling everyone back on set. Off you go, Sam.'

'Where've you been?' Georgia asked.

'Checking up on the script changes with the director. He wants yet more rewrites so before the cast turn on me en masse I think it might be a good idea if we make a run for it. The nurse asked me to thank you for your help. The poor woman is nearly going demented. You are not going to believe this but the leading man has developed chicken-pox. That's the reason his scenes are going to have to be rescheduled and I've got a mountain of rewrites to get through.

He'll be out of action for a while. We are going to have to film round him.'

'Does Belle know?'

'We are doing our best to keep the news from her. The nurse is going round with a questionnaire trying to work out who's open to infection and who isn't. No-one's plucked up the courage to ask Belle about her childhood illnesses. You wouldn't care to broach the subject at the cottage tonight? You know, in an informal atmosphere?' Dominic's suggestion died on his lips as he caught the look on Georgia's face. 'It was only an idea,' he said with a rueful smile.

'It was a bad one. Do you know she's accused Patsy of having fleas? I tell you one more word out of her and I'm sending her back to The Duck.'

'Don't do that.' Dominic looked alarmed. 'I'll have a word with her. See if I can air my diplomatic skills over a glass of that ghastly health drink she likes.'

'Are all shoots like this?' Georgia began to long for her cosy office back at the control centre.

'This one does seem to be suffering more than its usual number of set-backs,' Dominic admitted. 'No-one placed a curse on the manor, did they, after all that business with Sir John and William?'

'There's the Chile Pine. You know a monkey-puzzle tree? It got its name because even a monkey can't climb it.'

'You're not telling me there's another tree with a past about the place?'

'It's years old. I'll show it to you when you've got a spare moment.'

'I think I've already seen it,' Dominic said. 'One of the cameramen hacked a chunk off it a day or so ago. He couldn't get his equipment past it. I wondered why there was a bit of a fuss. Not bad luck, is it?'

''Fraid so.' Georgia smiled. 'At least it is with this one. I don't know the ins and outs, but everyone gives it a wide berth. Interfere with it at your peril.'

'And I thought we were living in the twenty-first century.' Dominic picked up his briefcase. 'Ready?'

'Where are we going?' Georgia asked.

'Back to The Highwayman. The new owners aren't ready to move in and they are quite happy for us to use the premises in the meantime. There'll a few days' indoor shooting now we're without a leading man.

Dominic made a gesture of annoyance. 'I've left my notes in Belle's caravan. You go on back to the car. I'll be with you in a few moments. Carry my briefcase would you?'

Staggering under the weight of Dominic's enormous flight-crew style cabin bag, Georgia eventually made it back to the cab. The few moments' wait for Dominic to reappear turned into half-an-hour. Georgia drummed her fingers on the steering wheel. Wishing she had brought something to read, Georgia fidgeted uncomfortably in her seat. A buzzing noise alerted her attention to her mobile. She frowned. The text was from Jake Shand.

Georgia jumped as Dominic tapped

on the driver's window before she had a chance to read it.

'Sorry to keep you waiting.' There was a grim set to his mouth as he said, 'You are not going to believe this. The cameraman who chopped a branch off your monkey puzzle tree?'

'What about him?'

'He's fallen off his camera stand and broken his leg. They've called for an ambulance.'

A Surprise Apology

'Have another sausage roll,' Dominic urged Georgia, 'or there are some cheese pasties if you prefer.'

Georgia accepted one of each. It had been a long time since her light breakfast of orange juice and coffee and she was hungry. After Dominic had broken the news of the latest catastrophe to hit the filming schedule, it was discovered Lady Annabel's costume was missing along with Sir Matthew's naval uniform.

'The driver's sat nav threw a wobbly and sent him to Gloucestershire. Don't ask,' he added as Georgia was about to demand how that had happened.

'What do we do now?' she asked.

'Head for The Highwayman as planned,' Dominic advised. 'I've snaffled some eats from the catering van. Make the most of it. It may be a long day.'

They were enjoying their impromptu

picnic, sitting at an antique oak table that had been delivered since their last visit to The Highwayman.

'I only hope we can use the premises.' Dominic unpeeled a banana. 'You don't think there really is anything to this monkey puzzle tree curse do you?'

'You're not letting things get to you, are you?' Georgia asked.

'Course not. Only,' he hesitated 'have you heard from Jake Shand recently?'

'He sent me a text.' Georgia searched round for her handbag. 'In all the excitement I forgot to read it.'

'I can tell you what it probably says.' Dominic watched her scroll down her missed messages.

'New Cabs have officially temporarily suspended operations,' Georgia read off the text.

'That's the one. They were the official carrier for the unit. Film companies are always looking to cut costs and Abe Shand provided the best deal money-wise. Now you can see why

I didn't want to lose you.'

Georgia blinked back at him. Any notion she had that Dominic's feelings for her were of a more personal nature died in an instant. Their relationship was purely professional. She had been foolish to think otherwise.

'I should be getting back to the control centre. Can you manage without me this afternoon?'

An expression she didn't understand flickered across Dominic's face.

'I have paid for your services in advance,' he reminded her.

'I know, but in the circumstances perhaps we could renegotiate? I mean, the situation has changed.'

'I don't think so,' Dominic replied. 'This latest news will create extra workload for your drivers and the demands on your time will be under more pressure than they already are.'

'Exactly.'

'And if you aren't in the office to deal with them, then someone else will, wouldn't you say?'

'That's not the point.'

Georgia knew her temperature was rising from the sensation of heat warming the back of her neck.

'I think it is. It's not Georgia Cabs who have gone out of business and Georgia Cabs pride themselves on their professionalism, don't they?'

'Of course.'

'Then all your existing customers come first.'

'Naturally.'

'I am an existing customer, aren't I?'

'I feel I ought to be in the office,' Georgia repeated stubbornly, but she could tell by the expression on Dominic's face that she was wasting her time.

'Then we must agree to differ and, as the customer is always right, I'm afraid that's the end of the matter. Now, if you've finished your lunch?'

Georgia's appetite deserted her and she pushed away the uneaten remains of her pasty.

'As you wish. I'll make some calls.' She stood up. 'And you can do whatever it is you came here to do.'

'Thank you,' he replied with the suggestion of a triumphant smile. 'I envisage being an hour or so, after which I'd like you to drive me back to The Duck while I take stock of the situation.'

Outside in the fresh air, Georgia took a deep breath. She wondered how her grandmother would have dealt with the situation.

'Georgia?' Ray answered her call on the first ring. 'Have you heard the news?'

'About New Cabs, yes.'

'It's as we suspected. We've received so many enquiries from their drivers about jobs, we're inundated.'

'You know the form, don't you?'

'Don't worry. I can handle it.'

Georgia did not like having to admit that Dominic appeared to be right. Ray was coping without her.

'How about New Cabs' customers? Are we getting much interest from them?'

'A little. I've commissioned some freelance workers to tide us over, but it seems most of New Cabs' regular clientele expected something like this might happen and had steadily been moving business away from them. Looking at our bookings over the past two weeks we have inherited some new accounts. How are things in the film world?'

After Georgia had updated him on the situation regarding the shoot and telling Ray she was at The Highwayman should he need her, she rang off and went in search of Dominic. She found him in the large lounge.

Dominic produced a sheet of paper. 'Now I've printed out my rewritten love scene between Katherine and James. I think it will work, but we're going to have to imagine the room is decorated and furnished in the Regency style. We're attending an evening soirée. You haven't been out in society very long and you are nervous. An orchestra is playing in the background. No-one knows of our attraction for each other. We're not even sure about it yet ourselves, as we've only met a couple of times.

'Tonight we have danced together under the watchful eye of a gaggle of society matrons. I am a tremendous catch. I am rich and handsome and half the scheming mamas in the county are after me for their daughter's hand in marriage. You, on the other hand, are a rather shy, inexperienced girl with no fortune. You are blindingly beautiful but unaware of the fact. Do you think you can carry it off?'

'I'm sorry?'

'Can you read for me?'

'You want me to act the part of Katherine?' Georgia asked in disbelief.

'Yes. I need to hear how the words sound. Normally Belle would do the run through, but she's not here and the leading man is currently in quarantine, so you'll have to do the female lead. I'll be James.'

'I've never acted in my life.'

Dominic paused. 'Would it help if I told you my character is not quite such a good catch as everybody thinks? He has a hidden agenda. His father has lost a lot of money in an investment that went disastrously wrong and as the heir to an almost non-existent estate I have been told to seduce you, because unbeknown to you, you are due to inherit a substantial trust fund on your eighteenth birthday. In modern parlance, I am a love rat.' Dominic nudged a copy of the script at her. 'You did say you weren't used to standing around all day doing nothing, didn't you?'

Suspecting that Dominic was enjoying her discomfiture, Georgia snatched up the script. The words were a jumbled mess before her eyes. All the time aware of Dominic's eyes on her, she flashed him a look of what she hoped was searing scorn.

'It says here the touch of your fingers on mine sets my heart racing madly.'

'An absolutely essential element in costume drama, wouldn't you say?'

Dominic moved in closer.

'Now, are you ready? Can you try to pretend you feel giddy looking at me?'

Georgia stiffened as Dominic slid a hand round her waist.

'Da di da di da.'

'What are you doing?'

'Attempting to set the mood. I am the orchestra.'

Dominic tightened the hold of his arm around her waist as he waltzed her across the room.

'I know young ladies didn't do the waltz in those days and that it was a scandal for a young man to hold an unmarried woman in his arms, but I want you to get the feel of things.'

'I suppose.' Georgia looked up into his eyes.

She hadn't expected Dominic to be quite such a good dancer. For a tall man wearing jungle boots, he was remarkably light on his feet. He guided her around the room with a gentleness that belied his size and his limp.

'You're looking less frosty already. Is

my charm working?' Dominic enquired. 'Steady.' He stumbled over his feet as Georgia drew up with a sharp intake of breath.

'Hadn't we better get on with the scene?'

To her annoyance she was forced to blink rapidly as yet again one of her contact lenses slipped.

'That's it,' he crowed, 'that's exactly the look I want, one of puzzled confusion. Now off you go.'

Trying for all she was worth to pretend she was a blushing ingénue, Georgia assumed the persona of the naïve beautiful heroine Katherine. With gentle innuendo the meaning was clear. Katherine was in love with James and despite his father's tyranny, he, too, was in love with the sweet gentle girl he was about to deceive.

The words tumbled from Georgia's lips as she tried to withstand Dominic's charm. The scene crackled with atmosphere and Georgia understood why Dominic had won awards for his work.

Under his guidance the characters became real human beings, people who possessed faults, good and bad points, weaknesses and kindnesses.

Dominic had pretended to guide Georgia to an alcove. 'I thought we could finish the scene away from the hawk-eyed chaperones.'

Before Georgia realised his intention her body was drawn closely into his and Dominic's lips descended on hers. Their touch set every part of her body tingling. Lacking the self-control to struggle, Georgia succumbed to his embrace, her head whirling.

'Whoops, sorry to interrupt.' A familiar voice behind them broke into the embrace. 'Hello, dears. How nice to see you both again. Don't mind me. I only came in to look for my glasses. Gulliver, come back here at once.'

The dog padded across the room and began to lick Georgia's hand.

'Would you both like a cup of tea? When you've finished in here, of course?'

Georgia turned bright red in the face as she broke away from Dominic's hold.

'Hello, Hilda.' Dominic beamed at her, not in the least fazed by the interruption. 'A cup of tea would be lovely. Don't you think so, darling?' He turned innocent eyes back to Georgia.

She glared at him, wishing she possessed her grandmother's fiery temperament and that she had the courage to tell him exactly what she thought of him and his offer of a cup of tea, but, not wanting to hurt Hilda's feelings, she forced herself to smile.

'Yes.' She lowered her voice in order that Hilda shouldn't hear. 'Pretending to be in love with you is very hard work and requires a lot of acting.'

* * *

'Members of the public are not allowed in here.' Georgia looked up from her computer screen as a sulky-faced Belle slumped into her office.

'Ray buzzed me in. I came to apologise.' She ran an embarrassed hand through her long blonde hair and tried to smile.

'You what?' Georgia gasped, not sure she had heard Belle correctly.

It wasn't the most elegant of reactions, but it was the best Georgia could come up with at short notice.

'I shouldn't have suggested Patsy had fleas,' Belle mumbled. 'It was very rude of me.'

'Um.' Georgia swallowed, temporarily lost for words.

'I don't normally do that sort of thing. Look,' Belle pulled back the neck of her blouse 'it's all cleared up, so no harm done. That is,' the uncertain look was back in her eyes 'if you'll accept my apology.'

'I understand.' Georgia did her best not to croak as she gathered her wits. 'You were under pressure and nobody likes being bitten.'

The sulky look disappeared off Belle's face. She smiled at Georgia.

'You're not just saying that?'

'No, I mean, yes, I mean the other way round. What I am trying to say is apology accepted.'

'Thanks for being so gracious about it.' Belle now put a hand up to her mouth and giggled. 'I have been a bit impossible, haven't I?'

Georgia carried on frowning, not quite understanding where this reinvented Belle was coming from.

'Dominic had a go at me last night,' she explained. 'Said I was turning into a monster and if I wasn't careful he would insist the lead role was re-cast. That made me sit up and think. Dominic holds serious sway on any production he works on and, with everyone being laid off for a few days, now would be an ideal opportunity to release me from my contract.'

'They can't do that, can they?' Georgia's reaction was one of outrage. Belle had her faults, but in Georgia's book a contract was binding and for once she was on Belle's side.

'They can do whatever they like. I

know I wasn't their first choice to play Katherine. Dominic was against the decision from the start. I think he still is. That's what is making me nervous. I so want to prove I can do the part. Plus I have difficulty learning lines. What with all the rewrites, well, I've been a bit of a wreck and I'm afraid I've been taking it out on you and everyone else.'

'I've got a tough skin.' Georgia leaned back in her swivel chair. 'So now you've apologised to me you're going to have to make things up with Sam.'

'Sam?'

'One of my drivers who acts as an extra. He was telling me he accidentally stood in your way during a shoot and you were less than gracious to him.'

Belle chewed on her lip.

'Sam will be OK if you put in a good word for him with your make-up girl. I think he's taken a shine to her.'

'Really? Consider it done. Phew, this apologising work is worse than going for an audition.'

'Don't worry, you've passed.'

'It's nice here.' Belle looked round Georgia's office.

Georgia removed a pile of files threatening to teeter off her desk on to the floor. 'That's not the adjective I'd use. I never seem to get round to putting anything away.'

'Everything is so normal.' Through the window they could hear Ray berating a driver who had turned up late. 'See what I mean?' Belle said. 'Things get a bit detached from reality in the film world and it's very easy to believe your own publicity.

'I think your cottage is lovely, too. I was so pleased to get away from The Duck. All anyone talks about there is the production and the landlord was so rude to me just because I told him his bath towels were scratchy.'

There was a trace of the old Belle in the look of outrage she directed at Georgia.

Georgia smirked. It was her private opinion that Belle had been lucky not to be thrown out on the spot.

Belle's smile broadened. 'The moment we drove up to your home I knew I would like it here. My grandmother used to live in a cottage in the country and it was like going back to my childhood. What was she like — your grandmother?'

'Fearsome,' Georgia replied, 'but we all loved her to bits.'

The two girls smiled at each other. 'Friends?' Belle ventured.

'Friends,' Georgia agreed.

A delicate flush tinged Belle's face. 'Do you mind if I ask you something?'

'That depends,' Georgia replied, hoping she hadn't reacted too hastily to Belle's overture of friendship.

'You and Max?'

'What about us?'

'I mean, I know you were engaged to him, but is there anything between you now?'

'I don't know what he has been saying to you, but our engagement is well and truly over.'

'I'm so pleased. I wasn't sure. I always thought it was you and Dominic, but he can be a bit tricky.'

Georgia held up a hand. 'Can you stop a moment, please? I'm not getting your gist.'

'Sorry. I told you I was a muddle head. What I'm trying to say is would you mind if Max and I got together?' Belle paused. 'Don't you think he is the most wonderful person on this earth? He's so kind and considerate.'

It was only with extreme difficulty that Georgia managed to stop her mouth from falling open.

'He told me how you and Dominic found him in my room with a bouquet of roses. He wanted to surprise me with them but it went wrong when he almost knocked himself out on my wardrobe.'

'It was a bit of a shock finding him there,' Georgia admitted.

'He's been making all sorts of suggestions, invitations to dinner, that sort of thing. I backtracked a bit because despite what you think of me, I wouldn't have entertained the idea if I thought you and he were together, although I admit

I was tempted. I think he's the nicest man I've ever met.'

Georgia suspected that the actress might be more than a match for her erstwhile fiancé and that perhaps at last he had met his equal. Belle she was sure would not stand idly by while he dated other women.

'If you want to go out with Max I won't stand in your way,' Georgia told her, adding, 'I should just advise you that Dominic Talbot and I are not an item, either.'

'You're not?' Belle's voice was a squeak of surprise. 'Everyone on the set thinks you are.'

'Then perhaps you'd put them right,' was Georgia's terse reply. 'Now I would like to get on with my work, if that is all right.'

'I can't.'

Georgia frowned.

'Can't what?'

'Tell anyone about you and Dominic.'

'Why not?'

'Half of them are in quarantine and

the ones who aren't have been temporarily stood down. Didn't you know?'

The call Georgia had received that morning via a third party had merely advised her that Dominic would not be requiring her services in the immediate future. Glad as she was to get back to office work, Georgia had felt resentful that Dominic couldn't have rung her personally.

After the script re-enactment at The Highwayman Dominic had seemed lost in his thoughts. The atmosphere between them grew tense and Georgia had been glad when Dominic suggested going back to The Duck after they had had their tea with Hilda.

'I've had chicken-pox so I'm low risk,' Belle was speaking again, 'but I've been told not to leave the area as I may be needed for costume fittings and other stuff. I suppose there's nothing I can do to help in the office?'

'No.' Georgia was firm on that one.

'Thought you'd say that. I don't blame you. I'm a bit of a disaster waiting to happen when it comes to paperwork.' Belle blew out her cheeks. 'It's only half-past ten in the morning and I'm bored stiff already. I can't go far because I'm on call. It's the pits.'

'You could read up on local history if you want to get a feel of the area? It might help you with your part. My dad is a bit of a history buff. You'll find several books in the cottage on the subject. I'm sure he wouldn't mind you borrowing one.'

'Would you like me to take Patsy for a run at lunch time?'

'I'd appreciate that.'

'If you need any shopping I'm good at that, too.'

'I'll make you out a list.'

Belle stood up. 'See you later then. Bye.'

Ray popped his head round the office door after Belle had departed.

'What was all that about?' he asked.

'You know, I'm not entirely sure,' Georgia admitted, 'but I think we're friends.'

'She's a nice girl. Hard to believe all those stories about her being a bit of a madam on set.'

'By the way, it seems filming has been suspended due to this outbreak of chicken-pox. Perhaps you'd put the word round? Hopefully no-one's infected but it's best everyone should know.'

'First flu now chicken-pox. Dod Stretton's really going through it,' Ray muttered as he returned to the outer office.

* * *

'I've had a marvellous idea,' Belle greeted Georgia that evening.

'Can I smell garlic?' Georgia sniffed.

'You can, and peppers and tomatoes. I make a mean moussaka. Are you hungry?'

'Ravenous.' Georgia's stomach rumbled.

'Good. It won't be long. Why don't you pour us a glass of red wine while I go and stir something? I don't normally eat garlic when I'm filming for obvious reasons, but it is a weakness of mine and you'll just love my signature dish. I had a Greek boyfriend a few years ago and he taught me how to make it.'

'Haven't you made rather a lot?' Georgia hovered in the kitchen doorway.

Belle was wearing a red and white checked apron and the work surface was cluttered with almost every utensil in Georgia's cupboard.

'I hope you don't mind but I invited Max to join us.'

Georgia poured out some wine. 'Fine,' she said.

'And Dominic,' Belle added in a quieter voice.

Georgia stopped pouring. 'You did what?'

'I had to make up numbers.' The expression in Belle's violet eyes looked disturbingly innocent as she met Georgia's.

'You wouldn't by any chance be trying to match-make?'

Belle avoided further eye contact by vigorously stirring a bubbling cheese sauce. 'The boys should be here soon. I said we'd go casual because they want to watch the football on the television. That all right with you?'

'Absolutely,' Georgia agreed limply, swallowing a large mouthful of red wine. 'I'd better freshen up as we're expecting guests.'

'Don't be too long,' Belle called after her. 'You haven't heard about my brilliant idea.'

'I'm not sure I can take another shock this soon,' Georgia called over her shoulder as she headed for the shower.

She heard the murmur of male voices as she emerged from her bedroom a quarter-of-an-hour later. Keen not to give the impression that she had made a special effort with her appearance for a casual supper date with Dominic, she decided to wear a simple white shirt and a floral print skirt.

Dominic Talbot was not the sort of man she was normally attracted to. He was dominant, on occasions scruffy, decisive and he liked his own way.

Georgia bit her lip. He was also a good person to have around in a crisis. She had seen the way he had helped Hilda when she had been worried about spending the night alone in The Highwayman, and he hadn't blamed Georgia for being foolish enough to leave the keys in her cab that night in Stretton Wood.

'There you are,' Belle greeted her as she pushed open the sitting-room door.

The television set flickered in the corner of the room. Two teams of excited players were running around a pitch, one or two of them with their shirts over their heads.

'Has someone scored?' she asked.

'We have.' Max crossed the room and kissed her casually on the cheek. 'I always liked you in that skirt. Didn't I buy it for you?'

Appalled, Georgia remembered it had been his choice. 'Did you? I'd quite forgotten.' She tried to brush off her gaffe. 'It was the first item of clothing that came to hand.'

'Supper's ready,' Belle trilled. 'Would you help me with the plates, Dominic?'

'That was a tactless thing to say,' Georgia hissed as the other two left the room.

'Sorry, I didn't think.' Max cast an anxious glance towards the kitchenette. 'Should I go and apologise?'

'No. It would probably only make things worse. Sit down. Not next to me, you silly thing.' She pushed him away. 'Over there on the sofa. Leave enough space for Belle to sit beside you and for goodness' sake don't make any more remarks about my appearance.'

'Right. Er, about the other day,' he began. 'I'm sorry about the mess I made with the flowers.'

'Best move on, don't you think?' Georgia patted some cushions back into shape and sat down on a squashy chair.

Her motive in pushing Max towards the sofa had been twofold. Dominic would be forced into occupying the other squashy chair and not try to sit next to her.

'Come on, you two,' Max bellowed. 'Half-time's over.'

'I can't sit here,' Dominic complained.

'Why not?' Georgia demanded.

Like her, he had dressed down in casual denim jeans and jacket with a checked shirt open at the neck.

'I can't see the match.'

'I don't want to see it.' Belle jumped up from the sofa. 'Max, help me push the two squashy chairs together.'

Quite how it happened Georgia wasn't sure, but moments later she was seated next to Dominic on the sofa. She glared at Belle, not convinced the manoeuvre hadn't been another of her artifices.

Sitting stiffly on the edge of the cushion she forked up a mouthful of moussaka. By the time everyone had finished eating the second half of the match was over. Max and Belle had been content to talk in lowered voices, neither of them seeming interested in what was happening on the pitch.

Dominic, for his part, had lounged easily against Georgia's rearranged cushions, a smile curving his lips as he took in her discomfort. As the referee blew his whistle, Dominic shifted closer to Georgia.

'You can relax now,' he teased her. 'We won.'

'I am perfectly relaxed,' Georgia replied.

'Not perched on the edge of the sofa like that you aren't.' Dominic put a hand around her shoulders and drew her back against the cushions. 'There, isn't that better?'

Georgia would have liked to wriggle away from him but she had a nasty suspicion Dominic might have wriggled up the sofa after her.

'You know, you really are a rotten liar,' he teased. 'Anyone would think you were nervous in my company.'

Georgia blinked then jerked away from Dominic.

'Belle.' She turned towards her. 'Before supper you said something about a good idea?'

Belle clapped her hands. 'I forgot. Yes, Max, move out of the way.'

Somehow or other their hands had become entwined while they were pretending to watch the football match.

'Now where did I put it? Ah, here it is.' She produced a booklet from under a pile of celebrity magazines.

'I've been reading this.'

'A history of Dod Stretton?' Max squinted at the cover. 'Shouldn't have taken you long.'

'It says here,' she flicked through a few pages, 'yes, here it is. As a cure for all ills, it was thought necessary to drink pure spring water from the forest.'

'Don't tell me.' Dominic stifled a groan. 'You're not going to suggest we trek out into the wilds to drink some of the stuff, are you?'

'I think it's a very good idea.' Belle beamed at him. 'You've got to admit things are going disastrously wrong with the shoot and, as filming has been suspended, we've all got time on our hands. Come on, Dominic,' she coaxed. 'It might be fun. You never know, you could enjoy yourself. You can supply us with a couple of cabs, can't you, Georgia?'

'I can, indeed,' Georgia replied. 'And old country myths don't scare me, although I quite understand Dominic's fears. So if he'd like to stay behind, I won't mind.'

The look Dominic threw her told Georgia her arrow had reached its target.

'All right, I'll come,' he said. 'But don't blame me if the whole thing's a disaster.'

Drama in the Woods

'Come on, deep breaths, get rid of all that stale air in your lungs.' Georgia skilfully sidestepped a muddy rut.

'Bet you were head girl at school.' Dominic yelped as an overgrown branch slapped him full in the face.

'Serves you right for grumbling,' Georgia retaliated.

'I thought this was supposed to be fun.'

'It is, and mind that rabbit hole,' Georgia added as Dominic sank to his knees in front of her.

With a muttered oath Dominic struggled to his feet.

'I can think of better ways of spending a Saturday afternoon than trudging through a forest for a drink of water.'

'Then you should have taken one of them.' Georgia smiled sweetly at him.

'You blackmailed me into coming.'

'No, I didn't. You came of your own free will.'

'With all the walking-wounded members of the cast thinking this excursion would be a great idea,' Dominic swished at some bracken with a branch he was using to steady himself, 'there was a mass exodus from The Duck.'

'I'm not surprised they all walked out on you. Are you always this grumpy?'

'I am not grumpy,' Dominic objected, before adding with a quirky smile, 'I suppose you wouldn't believe me if I said the real reason I came along was because I couldn't resist the chance of spending an afternoon in your delightful company?'

'You're right. I wouldn't.'

'Come on, you two. Keep up and stop bickering,' Max called back. 'Anyone would think the pair of you were an old married couple.'

'Are you sure we aren't lost?' Dominic's voice echoed through the trees. 'I'm beginning to suspect we are going round in circles. I'm sure I've seen that rabbit hole twice before.'

'Trust me,' Belle trilled, 'I know exactly where I'm going.'

'Which is more than can be said for the rest of us,' Dominic muttered as everyone shuffled along in her wake.

'If my memory serves me correctly,' Georgia raised her voice above the giggling and scuffling noises emanating from the younger members of the unit who seemed to have got bored looking for spring water and decided to set up an impromptu game of tag, 'Stretton Spring was right in the middle of the forest, as the crow flies that is.'

'You knew where it was all along?' Belle raised her voice in indignation as she looked up from her scribbled map. 'Why didn't you say so?'

'Sorry,' Georgia apologised, 'but nobody actually asked me.'

Ever since Belle had come up with the idea of visiting the spring, she and Max had used it as an excuse to huddle together to discuss details. Not wanting to play gooseberry, Georgia had let them get on with it while she caught up on her backlog of paperwork.

At first Dominic had been dismissive of the idea, claiming he didn't believe in local curses or the healing properties of fresh water. To Georgia's surprise the rest of the unit had taken to the idea with enthusiasm.

'Change of scenery will do everyone good,' one of the cameramen said as he put his name down. 'Even if I don't like the idea of another tree with attitude.'

'The Stretton Oak has been dormant for years,' Georgia had replied.

'Which is more than can be said for that monkey puzzle tree,' had been his crisp rejoinder.

'We could have done with your help earlier, Georgia,' Max chimed in. 'Belle's map resembles nothing I've seen so far. What on earth is that squiggle supposed to be?'

'I dropped my pen, all right?'

'What can you remember about the path down to the spring, Georgia?' Max ignored Belle's glare.

'Not much. It's been a while since my brother and I used to come up here and have a picnic during the school holidays.'

'It says in the book I borrowed from your father that we have to leave the footpath somewhere around here and head east. Did you remember to bring a compass, Max?' Belle asked.

'Don't be daft.'

'Anyone?' Belle threw the question at the group huddled around her. There was a general shaking of heads. 'Dominic? Can't you put a finger in the air or something to test our direction?'

'That's to see which way the wind is blowing, isn't it? Not much use in Stretton Wood.'

'Can't you suggest anything useful, Max?' Belle wasn't looking quite so enthusiastic about a walk in the forest as she had been an hour ago.

'I'm doing my best, but you know me and country matters. I can't tell a cow from a bull.'

'Hope no-one's wearing red,' Sam joked.

Georgia bent down and pulled back some of the undergrowth.

'There used to be a little green marker at the side of the path telling you which way to go.'

'There's no sign of it now.' Dominic bent down beside her and began rummaging around.

Georgia could feel the strength in his arms as he tugged at a bramble. 'Hey.' His face creased into a smile. 'Would you look at that?'

'What have you found?' Belle called over.

A speckled butterfly flapped its wings, startled at the disturbance.

'It's beautiful, isn't it?' Georgia watched the sunlight dapple the insect's wings.

Crouched beside Dominic it was as if they were only the two people in the wood. Georgia's heightened senses became acutely aware of the green smell of the surrounding foliage and the feel of the sun on her bare arms as a ray broke through a gap in the trees.

'Yes, it is,' Dominic agreed in a soft voice as he looked at her.

'My dad loves coming up here with his birdwatching friends.' A voice further down the line broke the spell between them.

'Perhaps we should have got a twitcher to guide us,' someone else chimed in.

Dominic's eyes didn't leave Georgia's face as the butterfly gave its wings a final flap and flew off.

'Can't anyone come up with a better suggestion?' Belle grumbled.

'Our leading lady is getting restless.' Dominic cast a look in her direction.

'Perhaps this wasn't such a good idea,' Georgia agreed.

'What say we split up and do our own thing?' Dominic suggested.

'We can't do that. Besides it was you who wanted to get a feel of Stretton Wood for your research and that's exactly what you are getting — local colour.'

'This isn't quite what I had in mind.'

'Alice didn't let falling down a rabbit hole deter her. You can't chicken out now.'

'Why do you always have a smart answer for everything?'

Georgia could feel Dominic's breath on her face as he leaned towards her.

'Because she's the boss.' Sam appeared from behind the Stretton Oak, hand in hand with the make-up girl.

'Didn't anyone tell you it's rude to eavesdrop?' Dominic demanded, easing back slightly.

''Spect so.' Sam didn't look in the least abashed by the put down. 'But it's a marvellous way to learn what's going on.'

'You should train your staff better.' Dominic stood up, abandoning his search for the green marker.

Georgia tweaked a bit of branch out of his hair. 'In case you hadn't noticed we are getting left behind.'

Sam and the others were now out of sight.

'Scared to be alone with me in an

enchanted forest?' Dominic taunted and circled his fingers round her wrist.

Above them a bird flapped its wings in the trees. A cascade of leaves descended.

'Now you're covered in bits of twig.' Georgia was determined not to flinch at the intensity of feeling in Dominic's eyes.

'Then why don't you remove them?'

'Because you're old enough to comb your own hair.'

A shaft of sunlight caught the star-shaped scar on his forehead.

'Come on then.' To Georgia's relief Dominic let go of her wrist, but her relief was short lived. 'Look out.'

If he hadn't yanked her away from a protruding tree root she would have gone sprawling. He encircled her body in his arms and crammed her cowboy hat back on her head. She tried to wriggle away from him.

'Steady,' he protested. 'We can't take any chances. With so many disasters befalling the unit it's as well to be careful. We don't want any more broken bones.'

'Max thinks it's this way,' Belle announced from up the front. 'Hurry up, stragglers.'

They plunged deeper into the forest. Twigs cracked under the onslaught of their boots and Georgia heard one or two muttered curses as people slipped on the mud.

'It's getting awfully dark.' Belle complained after they had been going for several minutes. 'Max, I don't like it. It's spooky.'

'Stop whinging.'

'Before we have a full blown tantrum on our hands,' Dominic murmured in Georgia's ear, 'can't you remember anything helpful from your childhood forays into the forest?'

The atmosphere grew danker and gloomier and it began to hurt to breathe.

'I'm beginning to suspect Max is right and we are going in the wrong direction,' Georgia said.

'Fancy telling our leader that gem?'

'I think I can hear running water,' Max announced.

'It's coming from over here.' Belle made an excited rush forward.

'Steady on.' Max raced after her. 'Don't slip in those shoes. I told you not to wear heels. You'll twist your ankle.'

'Come on. We'd better follow everyone. What exactly are we supposed to do when we get to this water source?' Dominic demanded.

'What do you think? Drink some, of course.'

'All the natural spring water I've tasted has never done anything for me.'

'It's supposed to possess restorative powers,' Georgia said.

'Well, if it can cure my dodgy knee then I'm up for it. Don't worry.' He grinned at the consternation on Georgia's face as she remembered how she had laughed when he had fallen to his knees. 'It would take more than a rabbit hole to jar it.'

'I'm sorry. I keep forgetting. How did you injure it?'

After a few moments and just as Georgia was beginning to think he wasn't going to answer her question, Dominic said, 'I wasn't looking where I was going and I tripped over a cable, bashed my head,' he indicated the scar in the middle of his forehead, 'and landed on my knee. I felt it crack as I went down. I was in plaster for six weeks. That's why I'm too lazy to walk everywhere and need the services of a personal driver. Please,' Dominic held up a hand, 'no sympathy by request, not that you were going to offer any, I suspect,' he said, a rueful smile quirking a corner of his mouth. 'I paid the price for a moment's inattention.'

'Dominic?' one of the cameramen called him over. 'Want me to take some pictures with my digital? You could put them on your laptop when we get back to The Duck. It might help your research.'

'If we ever get back.' Dominic loped

over to where a small group of technicians were standing.

'It's not true, you know,' Sam murmured to Georgia.

'What?'

'That story about how he damaged his knee.'

'You mean he lied?' Georgia caught her breath in surprise.

'Sort of. He did trip and bang his head, but the reason he wasn't paying attention was because he was rescuing some children who were in danger of walking into an ambush. I don't know all the details, but it was somewhere in Africa, I think. He was out there helping with a documentary and the children were naturally curious. If it hadn't been for his quick reaction I dread to think what might have happened.' Sam glanced over his shoulder. 'He's coming back.'

'What's Sam looking so furtive about?' Dominic demanded as he scuttled off.

'Just a bit of gossip,' Georgia improvised.

Georgia decided it had to be the

intermittent sunlight through the leaves that was turning Dominic's eyes such an unusual soft shade of blue.

'Dominic.' Belle appeared from nowhere and tugged at his elbow. 'I need your help. Max is useless. He led us all into a dead-end clearing.'

She smiled prettily at both of them. When neither Dominic nor Georgia took any notice, Belle narrowed her eyes.

'Up to your old tricks with the hired help, Dominic?' she challenged him. When her words still provoked no reaction, Belle dropped her hold on Dominic's arm. 'I can see where I'm not wanted. Don't come crying to me, Georgia, when you're dumped.'

Pouting, she flounced off. Before Georgia could speak they heard raised voices in the distance. Patsy began to bark excitedly.

'Belle, where are you?' Max called out. 'We really have found our spring this time.'

'You'd better be right,' she replied.

Dominic squeezed Georgia's fingers.

'That's the best news I've heard all day. Come on.'

'Whatever Max has found, Patsy seems to be making a lot of noise about it,' Georgia panted a few moments later as she and Dominic avoided yet another deep puddle of slimy mud.

Dominic increased his pace. 'It sounds urgent to me.'

'Is that Belle screaming?' Georgia asked.

'I think she's in trouble. Come on.'

'You go on ahead.' Georgia grabbed at her side. 'I've got a stitch. I'm fine, I'll catch up.' She gasped.

Dominic disappeared in the direction of all the noise. Breathing heavily behind him Georgia emerged into the clearing a few moments later to be confronted by chaos. People were running to and fro, shouting, several others were standing on the edge of the waterfall peering over.

'What happened?' Georgia snatched at Sam's sleeve.

'Belle's fallen in the water. There.' He

pointed. 'She slid on some mud and her feet went from under her.'

'I can't swim.' Max grabbed Dominic by the shoulders. 'Do something. She's going to drown.'

Kicking off his boots Dominic plunged into the water. The level was high and the current dragged him to his knees to where Belle was face down in the shallows. Putting his hands under her armpits he dragged her free from the reeds.

'Is she breathing?' Max gasped.

'Someone call an ambulance!' Sam shouted

'Patsy, come back,' Georgia shrieked. Her feet began to slip underneath her as she ran after a thoroughly over-excited Patsy who was racing along the path caught up in the mayhem.

Moments later Georgia, too, had slipped off the bank and into the water. She staggered to her feet and made a grab at a ball of wet fur.

'Patsy, here.'

The dog paddled furiously as the

current caught her and carried her off downstream. Through a haze of noise and panic Georgia felt a strong pair or arms drag her out of the water.

'It's OK.' One of the security guards put her down on the grass. 'Sam's got your dog.'

Georgia began to shiver as a wet Patsy licked her face. She stroked the soaking ears and began to sob in relief.

'Where's Belle?' She took several deep gulps.

The group of bystanders parted to reveal Dominic on his knees beside a recumbent Belle.

He breathed another mouthful of air into her lungs as he administered the kiss of life, a look of anguish on his face.

'She's not breathing.' He gasped. 'Where the blazes is that ambulance?'

Confessions of Love

'It's official,' Ray announced, 'about New Cabs. Abe Shand has put up the shutters. Are you feeling OK?' He frowned, taking in the dark circles under Georgia's eyes and her pale complexion.

'Yes. Sorry. Haven't been sleeping well lately.'

'Twelve hour days with no breaks aren't good for you.'

'What was that about Abe Shand?' Georgia had no wish to be drawn into a discussion on the matter.

'He's thrown in the towel,' Ray replied, 'and I think he wants to arrange a meeting regarding the possibility of us salvaging what's left of his business.'

'I'll be pleased to help in any way I can, but there's only so much I can do. My father is still head of the business.'

'That's what I tried to tell him, but I don't think he was listening. He said something about not being available personally, but he would send over a representative later in the day.'

'Keep me posted if there are any developments.'

'Will do. There's a pile of paperwork on your desk needing urgent attention. Have a nice day.' Ray grinned.

A bout of hard work was exactly what Georgia needed to help her forget Stretton Wood. The look on Dominic's face as he cradled Belle in his arms, murmuring endearments into her ear after successfully breathing life back into her lungs, was enough to convince Georgia he was in love with Belle. They must have had a falling out when they were on holiday in the Caribbean and he had used Georgia in much the same way as Belle had used Max. Her lips tightened. As far as Georgia was concerned they deserved each other.

Sam had driven the cab back to the control centre and Georgia had taken the people carrier back to The Duck after the ambulance had taken Belle and Dominic to the hospital. Belle had clung on to Dominic and sobbed into his shoulder, begging him not to leave her side. And he hadn't. Belle hadn't returned to Dod Cottage and her bed hadn't been slept in for several days now. There had been no word from Dominic.

Georgia had to get him out of her mind. He was a successful international scriptwriter who travelled all over the world at a moment's notice. There was no common ground between them. From now on her work was going to be her life and if her father decided to settle in Australia, then she would be more than happy to take complete control of the business.

'Hello, Georgia.'

She looked up from checking her emails. 'Jake?'

He was standing in the doorway to her office, his eyes etched with tiredness. He didn't look as though he had combed his hair and his clothes were rumpled.

'Long time, no see,' he said.

'Where have you been?' Georgia asked.

'Afraid to show my face,' he admitted with an embarrassed smile. 'Mind if I sit down?'

'Of course not.' Georgia was half way out of her seat to help him, but Jake waved her away.

'I can manage,' he insisted.

'I'm so sorry about New Cabs.'

'I'm not.'

This was a Jake Georgia didn't recognise. It was as if he had grown up since she had last seen him. 'My father's a hard-headed businessman. He'll resurface. He's good at that. It's the employees I feel sorry for, but Ray says you'll take the drivers on?'

'Well.' Georgia hesitated, unwilling to commit herself. 'I can't make any promises.'

'I can give the good ones references and the business is sound. Dad drummed up lots of new accounts.'

'And he poached some of ours,'

Georgia reminded Jake. 'I can't quote the same rates.' She paused. 'Did your father send you over to negotiate?'

'I volunteered. I wanted to talk to you, to apologise and try to explain things.'

There had been so much happening over the past few weeks that Georgia couldn't remember when she had last seen Jake. At one time he had been a permanent fixture around the control centre, but after the business at The Highwayman he hadn't been around so much.

Jake took a deep breath. 'I did sabotage cab number six on purpose.' He held up a hand before Georgia could intervene. 'I haven't finished. I knew what I'd done to cab six wasn't too serious and any competent mechanic could sort it out.' He swallowed.

'Sabotaging cab number six.' Georgia saw no reason to go easy on Jake.

'Right.' Jake breathed. 'I also have to tell you I probably could have caught up with Dominic that day when he left his briefcase in the back of my cab.'

'Then why didn't you?'

'It's difficult to say, but if I hadn't done anything at all my father's suspicions would have been alerted. You must have suspected I was a mole? I was supposed to infiltrate Georgia Cabs and, well, you know what moles do.'

'And you thought a lost briefcase and filling a car with poor petrol would do the trick?'

'It seemed the easiest option. I also suggested to some of your customers that they could contact New Cabs if they wanted a better rate, that sort of thing. My father wanted me to do lots of other stuff, serious things, but I wouldn't hear of it. Am I making sense?'

'So your father really did use you as a plant because he wanted to put Georgia Cabs out of business?'

The expression on Jake's face was enough to convince Georgia her suspicions were correct.

'He doesn't like competition and he

knew Georgia Cabs had a good reputation. With your parents away in Australia, and with you in charge of things in their absence, he sensed a walkover. I know,' Jake raised a hand 'I could have wised him up on that one. When it comes to business you're up there with the best of them. I contented myself with handing out some of his cards to your customers and giving them a bit of sales talk. After that business at The Highwayman I was frantic with worry. I really thought something serious had happened to you and I wanted out.'

'So you decided to make yourself scarce?'

Jake nodded.

'I enjoy my work at the garage. It's nothing to do with dad, and I am my own man there, but I knew if I hung around here my father would start suggesting all sorts of mad schemes again, so I went away for a bit to try to get my head together.

'I'm sorry. I know you'll think badly

of me and I can never make up for the damage I've done, but that's an end to it, I promise you.'

Outside on the forecourt Georgia could hear one of her drivers calling to another over the crackle of a radio. Petrol fumes wafted through the open window as an engine was started up.

'Georgia?' Jake prompted when she didn't speak.

She cleared her throat. 'I think,' she began with a smile, 'that you've been incredibly brave.'

Jake frowned. 'I don't follow.'

'It takes courage to own up and you haven't tried to make excuses for what you did.'

A look of relief spread over Jake's face. His cheeks were still ruddy from the discomfort of his confession.

'You don't know how pleased I am to hear you say that. I've been so worried. I didn't sleep a wink all night. I'm trying to do my best by everybody, but my father left things in quite a mess. He's asked me to handle the handover if you accept his offer.'

'I can't make a decision right now, but I'm sure it will all get sorted out eventually.'

'So where do we go from here?'

'I'll conference call my father in Australia. We can't do anything until he returns.'

'I understand.' Jake stood up. 'I won't take up any more of your time. Thanks for listening to me and thanks for being so great about things. I really do appreciate it.' He paused by the door. 'By the way I'm a bit out of touch. How have things been going with the film people?'

'Didn't you know filming has been suspended due to an outbreak of chicken-pox?'

'No, really?' Jake raised his eyebrows. 'Dad had a lot riding on that deal. I expect that's what sent the business plummeting. Sorry things didn't work out between you and Dominic.' Jake said. 'Though it doesn't matter now.'

The telephone on Georgia's desk jangled into life.

'You'd better take the call. It could be from one of New Cab's dissatisfied customers. Tell them I apologise and that it's business as normal with Georgia Cabs.'

'What do you mean?' Georgia ignored the call. 'About things not mattering now with Dominic?'

'I caught the tail end of a newsflash on the radio as I was driving over.'

Through the glass window of her office Georgia could see Ray making agitated gestures at her to pick up the telephone. She ignored him.

Jake hesitated as if he were having difficulty choosing his words.

'Dominic Talbot on line one.' Ray elbowed him out of the doorway. 'Sorry to interrupt, Jake, but Dominic did say it was urgent.'

'Tell him I'm totally tied up with New Cabs today. I can schedule him another driver if it's an emergency, but I need to be on call here.'

'Well, see you around.' Jake waved at her.

'No, Jake, don't go.'

'I don't think Dominic wants a driver.' Ray stood his ground. 'Filming has been suspended indefinitely.'

'That's old news and, as filming has been suspended, I can think of no reason why Dominic would wish to speak to me and I have no reason to speak to him ever again.'

'Anything you say.' Ray returned to the switchboard in the control centre.

'Don't be too harsh on him,' Jake said. 'Belle's a beautiful girl and film people are different from the likes of you and me.'

'Jake, what are you talking about?'

'Belle Jeffreys. It was on the radio this morning. She's married.'

* * *

Georgia tried to focus on her figure work after Jake had delivered his killer parting shot, but the numbers wouldn't make sense.

Back at the cottage Georgia made a

milky drink then, turning off the telephone, she took the drink up to her room and fell asleep the moment her head touched the pillow.

The banging on the door wouldn't go away. Georgia rolled over and opened one eye. She had tumbled into a deep sleep on top of the bed leaving her clothes in a crumpled heap on the floor.

Whoever had been banging at the door was now attacking the bell with vigour. She could hear Patsy barking excitedly down in the conservatory. Rolling off the bed Georgia slowly got to her feet, hoping her head would clear and that the ringing on the doorbell would soon stop.

Through the frosted glass of the door she could make out the blurred shape of a man's head.

'Who's there?' she called out.

'It's me, Jake.'

Georgia unlocked the chain and peered round the crack. She recoiled as the biggest bunch of flowers she had ever seen in her life confronted her.

'Jake?' She sneezed as pollen irritated her nostrils.

'Peace offering.' His voice came from somewhere within the depths of an orange chrysanthemum.

'You've already done that bit yesterday. There was no need to buy me a bouquet.'

'Yes, there is,' Jake insisted. 'I don't know what came over me. Back in the car I realised I shouldn't have done it. You were good to me and I paid you back by being a rat.'

'I think I need some coffee,' Georgia said, deciding she really couldn't ask Jake to garble his explanation again.

'Good idea. I'll join you. Want to freshen up while I make it?' Jake was in the hall before Georgia could prevent him entering the cottage.

Georgia remained under the shower for fifteen minutes, alternating the water between hot and cold sprays. She relished the relief of the needlepoint jets on her flesh. Now she was getting her head together she had to remind herself sharply that she absolutely would not waste any more time thinking about Dominic Talbot. Whatever Jake had done, he could not be as big a rat.

'I was beginning to think you'd gone back to sleep.' Jake looked up from the table. 'I've seen to Patsy and settled her down in her basket.' There was a gentle snore from a corner of the kitchen, 'and I've put the flowers in water. There.' He pointed to the sink. 'I couldn't find a vase.'

'I'm not sure I could find one, either. I'm not used to receiving flowers from gentlemen callers.' Georgia smiled at him. 'Thank you, a lovely gesture, but totally unnecessary.'

Jake nudged the percolator towards her. 'I made it hot and extra strong. You look as though you need it.'

Georgia savoured the aroma of the fresh coffee as she poured herself a cup and took a sip.

'Better?' Jake smiled.

'Better,' Georgia nodded. 'I crashed out last night,' she admitted. 'It's been quite a week and things caught up with me.'

Another loud ring on the doorbell made them both jump.

'Are you expecting anyone?' Jake sounded annoyed at the interruption.

'I don't think so,' Georgia replied.

'Then don't answer it.'

'Don't be ridiculous, Jake. Of course I have to answer it. It could be important.'

'Nothing's as important as what I have to say to you.'

He put a hand across the table and gripped Georgia's wrist as she tried to stand up.

'Jake, stop it.' Georgia began to grow annoyed. She struggled to free herself from his hold then froze at the sound of a key being inserted into the lock.

'Hello?' A voice called down the corridor. 'It's only me.' A shadow appeared in the doorway. 'Hope you don't mind, Georgia. I let myself in with Belle's key. I won't make a habit of it I promise. In fact, you can have it back. She won't be needing it any more.'

'Max?'

'Whoops, sorry. Have I interrupted something?' He looked down to where Jake was still clutching Georgia's hand.

Taking advantage of Jake's diverted attention Georgia leapt to her feet and ran towards Max, kissing him on the cheek.

'Whoa!' He laughed. 'You'll crush my blooms.'

It was then Georgia noticed Max was also holding a bunch of flowers.

'For you.' He thrust them at her.

'Max, I'm so sorry.' Georgia squeezed his arm. 'I know how you felt about Belle,' she began. 'You must be gutted.'

'Nothing to be sorry about,' he insisted. 'In fact, you should be congratulating me, shouldn't you?' he asked with a perplexed frown. 'Or have we both lost the plot?'

Georgia took a step back from Max and stared at him in confusion.

'You mean you're pleased?'

'Of course I'm pleased. Who wouldn't I be?'

'That's what I've been trying to tell

you.' Jake sidled round the table and tried to muscle in between them.

Max ignored him. 'Belle sent me over to pick up one or two of her things, if that's all right with you, Georgia? Only a day's honeymoon for her, I'm afraid. After filming is finished we'll probably fix up a decent holiday, somewhere warm with miles of sandy beaches and blue skies.'

'You and Belle are planning a holiday?' Georgia blinked at him.

'When we can get a window. Georgia?' Max still looked puzzled. 'You're very pale. Aren't you feeling well?'

'You and Belle. It's all over between you, isn't it?' she asked uncertainly.

Max laughed. 'You don't know? You haven't heard? That explains it. I know we behaved badly at the spring, didn't we? Truth is we'd had a bit of a row. I didn't think someone like Belle would want to get married. She's a serious career girl, after all. I wasn't even sure I wanted to settle down, either, but I'm the first to admit I was wrong. When I saw Dominic leap into the water to rescue Belle, then start giving her the kiss of life, I realised what I had very nearly lost and that I couldn't live without her. So after she'd been checked out at the hospital and given the all clear, we raced off and, well, to cut a long story short, Belle is now Mrs Doyle.'

Georgia turned from Max to look at Jake.

'There wasn't time to tell anyone of our plans. Belle felt badly about not contacting you. She guessed you would be worried so she sent me over to apologise. The flowers are really from her, not me. She said to tell you she hopes to call in later to give you all the girly details. I've left her with Dominic in the dining-room of The Duck, huddled over yet more script rewrites. They've re-cast the leading man, did you know? So the production is on again.'

Max ground to a halt as he took in the expression on Georgia's face, then he leant forward and kissed her hair.

'What a brute I am. All this must have come as a bit of a shock to you. If I've hurt you, Georgia, I'm really sorry, but I do love Belle and I think the reason things didn't work out between you and me was because a part of me sensed we weren't suited.'

'You knew?' Georgia accused Jake as she pushed Max away. 'That's what the flowers are all about, isn't it? You deliberately misled me.'

Max's smile faltered. 'Am I missing something here?' he asked.

'It was a moment's madness,' Jake replied.

'What was?' Max demanded.

'I let Georgia think it was Dominic and Belle who eloped.'

'You did what?' Max shouted. 'Why?'

'I thought, maybe, I don't know.' He shrugged. 'It was totally out of character. I've always hoped Georgia and I,' Jake turned back to Georgia, 'well, you know how I felt about you, and I thought if you believed Dominic was permanently out of the way maybe we could get together. Stupid, I realise that now, especially after you'd been so good to me about everything, besides, sooner or later, you were bound to find out the truth. Sorry, Georgia. Can you ever forgive me?'

Max dropped his flowers on the table and as Georgia swayed he caught her in his arms.

'Quick, Jake, a chair.'

Georgia sank on to it. Max began rubbing her hands.

'Open a window, get some air in here,' he barked another order at Jake who, anxious to make amends, promptly did as he was told.

'Here, have some coffee,' Jake offered.

'I don't want any coffee.' Georgia shook her head. 'I want you all to leave me alone.'

Max brushed damp hair off her forehead. 'I'm not going anywhere with you like this.'

'If you want to get back to Belle, I'll stay on,' Jake offered.

'I should imagine you are the last person Georgia wants in her life at the moment.' Max glared up at him. 'You and your father have really messed up her life.'

'What about you?' Jake retaliated. 'You haven't exactly behaved like a gentleman.'

'At least I had her interests at heart. Get out, go on.'

'I'm not going anywhere. Stop shoving me.'

Patsy began to bark and run round in excited circles as Georgia tried to remonstrate with the two men.

'For goodness' sake, I've been hammering on the door for ages hoping someone would come and answer it.' Ray barged into the kitchen. 'I couldn't get through on the telephone, either.'

'I turned the bell off before I fell asleep last night,' Georgia admitted swaying against Max.

'What is going on?'

'Hello, Ray,' Max greeted him. 'Join the party. Glad you've arrived. You're just in time to stop me throttling Jake Shand.'

'Whatever it is you two are arguing about, you're making enough noise to raise the whole of Dod Stretton.'

'This idiot here,' Max began to explain, 'told Georgia it was Dominic who eloped with Belle.'

'That's not strictly true.'

'You are not going to believe this,' Max carried on, 'but he had some idea of getting together with Georgia. I mean, in your dreams, Jake. Anyway, when she found out it was Belle and I who are married,' he waved a hand towards the mess, 'this was the result.'

Ray looked round the cramped kitchen. Patsy had now begun to growl and tug at Max's bunch of flowers that in all the confusion had slipped off the table. Petals floated in pools of spilt coffee alongside a packet of soggy biscuits that had also fallen to the floor. Patsy pounced on the crumbs and began demolishing what remained of the custard creams.

'I think,' Ray's voice injected some authority into the situation, 'that you had all better leave.'

Jake and Max raised their voices in protest.

'Now,' he insisted.

'Come on then, Shand,' Max said. 'Georgia wants to be left alone. Sorry, darling.' He leaned forward and kissed her tenderly on the forehead. 'I'm always here for you, you know that?'

There was a further movement behind him in the doorway. Over Max's left shoulder Georgia's eyes clashed into those of Dominic's.

'Dominic,' Ray apologised. 'Sorry. I forgot about you. I left him standing on your doorstep,' he explained to Georgia. 'We both came to see how you were getting on as we couldn't get through on the telephone. Dominic wasn't sure he would be welcome so I told him to stay put while I sussed things out.'

A bubble of laughter erupted in Georgia's throat as she realised Dominic, too, was carrying a bunch of flowers.

'Pink carnations?' She raised an eyebrow.

She hardly noticed Ray usher Max and Jake out of the kitchen.

'I remembered you telling me they are your favourite flowers,' Dominic said in a soft voice. 'Now everyone else has gone may I come in?'

* * *

Georgia and Dominic sat side by side on canvas-backed seats that Dominic had acquired from the film set. The remains of their lunch were strewn on a picnic rug under their feet. In the background Georgia took comfort from the sound of the waterfall as it trickled into the fast running stream.

'Do you want to go first?' Dominic asked. 'You look as though you have a lot to get off your chest.'

Georgia lost the brief battle with her conscience that tried to tell her she didn't care what Dominic got up to with the women in his life.

'The last time I saw you, you were cradling Belle Jeffreys in your arms.'

'Is that why you refused to take my telephone calls?' Dominic raised his eyebrows in surprise. 'I was rescuing her. Max can't swim. What was I supposed to do?'

'You were whispering endearments and kissing her.'

'Mouth to mouth resuscitation, actually.'

'In her ear?'

Dominic acknowledged the correction with a nod of his head. 'I admit I did brush my lips over her earlobe, but only because I was so relieved she hadn't actually passed out on me. I would have got back to you sooner only I was called to London for urgent re-casting meetings. Belle, well, she had other things on her mind. It was only when we all met up again this morning that we realised you were still in the dark as to what was going on.'

Georgia still wasn't totally sure she believed Dominic's explanation but before she could say anything, Dominic went on, 'I didn't realise Belle's act at the waterfall was all part of a clever ruse on her part to get her own back on Max. He'd turned down her marriage proposal or something the night before and they'd had words. That's why they were carping at each other all the way up here.' Dominic rubbed at his knee in an abstracted manner. He cast a sideways glance at Georgia. 'We've got better things to talk about than those two.'

'Have we?' Georgia feigned interest in the last strawberry.

'Put that thing down,' Dominic knocked it out of her hand, 'and listen to me.'

'Dominic,' she protested as Patsy raced after the piece of fallen fruit. 'That wasn't very polite.'

'I don't feel like being polite at the moment. In fact I feel like behaving rather badly.'

He leaned in towards her. A blush began to work its way up Georgia's neck.

Dominic picked up a paper cup and pulled Georgia to her feet.

'Where are we going?'

'This was your idea, wasn't it?'

'What was?'

'To drink some pure spring water?'

'It was Belle who first suggested it.'

'So that's what we are going to do.' Dominic ignored the correction.

'You said it tasted peculiar.'

'I also recall it's supposed to be a cure for all ills.'

They were now leaning over the edge of the waterfall. Georgia could feel the strain of Dominic's body against hers.

'Steady.' She grasped out at him.

'Got it,' he said in triumph as water splashed into his cup. 'I'm not sure if this is the source of the stream, but it'll serve our purposes. Here.'

He nudged the rim of the cup against Georgia's lips. 'Drink up.'

'I'm not ill,' she protested.

'I am.'

'What?' She coughed as a mouthful of water went down the wrong way.

Dominic thumped her on the back. 'Better?'

'What's wrong with you?' She gasped.

'I'm not sure.' Dominic took the cup from her unresisting fingers. 'But I think the technical term is that I've fallen in love.'

'With who?' Georgia spluttered.

'You, of course, who else?'

Dominic wiped away the moisture trickling down her wet cheeks.

'Are you saying you're in love with me?' Georgia's voice was a hoarse rasp.

'It doesn't seem to be doing a very good job on your voice, either.' Dominic looked down at the nearly empty cup. 'Its restorative powers are decidedly lacking. Didn't quite catch what you said.' He looked expectantly at Georgia. 'Would you mind repeating yourself?'

'Are you in love with me?' Georgia hadn't meant to shout and she winced as her voice echoed round the glade.

'Hmm, well that certainly frightened the birds out of the trees. Maybe this stuff does work after all.'

'Answer my question,' Georgia insisted with a stubborn set to her jaw.

Dominic took a slow deliberate sip of the water then grimaced. 'I was right. It's too cold. Sets my teeth on edge.' He turned to face her with a smile that set Georgia's pulses racing. 'I've been in love with you from the moment I first saw you,' he said.

'In the control centre?'

'I could see you were dying to give me a piece of your mind for being so rude to you about my misplaced briefcase. I know it wasn't very gallant of me, but I wanted to see how far I could push you before you blew a fuse.'

'Of all the underhand dirty tricks,' Georgia spluttered, 'that takes the biscuit.'

'Is it too late to say sorry?'

'Far too late.'

'And?' Dominic looked at her expectantly.

'And what?' Georgia asked carefully.

'Has the water worked its magic on you? I know I don't deserve your love, but with Max happily married and Jake slinking off the scene with his tail between his legs, am I in with a chance?'

Georgia's heartbeat was beating a military tattoo as she looked into Dominic's blue eyes.

'To be honest I think you are the most stubborn, difficult, infuriating man I have ever met, and drinking a cup of water will not change my opinion of you.'

'I see. Is that it? Anything else you'd like to off-load while you're at it? As a character assassination I'd say it's going pretty well.'

'Film people appear to be the craziest people I have ever met in my life. You've all got enormous egos. You're self centred, totally unreliable and think the world revolves around you.'

'Yup, that about sums us up nicely. We do work hard though and I hope our work brings pleasure to a lot of people.' Dominic circled his arms around Georgia's waist. 'I've bought The Highwayman.'

'You've done what?' Georgia stopped mid flow.

'The new people's funding never came through. They've dropped out of the deal. Hilda was telling me all about it last time we were up there.

'That's what gave me the idea. I've been looking to put down permanent roots for a while. I thought I could turn The Highwayman into a centre for performing arts. There's a lot going on round here. It would be an ideal location.'

'You're coming to live in Dod Stretton?'

'I've had enough of travelling around the world and I knew you'd never leave here, especially not if you take over the family business. It wouldn't be fair of me to expect it. I couldn't ask you to share my previously crazy lifestyle so I decided I could join you instead, if you want me to.'

Georgia's head was swimming.

'I think I need to sit down.'

'Not until you've told me what you think of the idea.'

Dominic placed firm hands on

Georgia's shoulders.

'If you really can't bear The Highwayman, I could try and outbid Max's outfit for Dod Manor, but I think they're pretty well-established and I couldn't be too sure of a successful outcome, besides there's that wretched monkey puzzle tree. I don't want it putting a curse on me every time I mow the lawn. So what's your answer to my question?' he asked with a slow smile.

'What question?' Georgia's vision was beginning to blur.

'Also, I hate to sound picky, but you haven't actually said you loved me. I mean it would help matters if you did.'

'Love you?' Georgia echoed. 'Of course I love you, that's why I'm so mad at you.'

'You mean it?' A slow smile spread across Dominic's face. 'I never thought I'd hear you say those words. Every time we met up it was one disaster after another. I did my best to convince you there was nothing between Belle and me, but I just couldn't get my act together and when Belle wasn't creating waves there was Max hovering about in the background, taking you out to dinner.'

'He was proposing a business venture.'

'How was I to know that? The man was a perfect pest. I half thought those flowers were for you the day we caught him flat out on the floor in Belle's room. I was so relieved when you said your favourite flowers were pink carnations.'

'Is that why you bought me a bunch today?' Georgia asked with a warm feeling in the pit of her stomach.

'I had to ring round half the countryside to find some fresh ones. It took me ages to locate any. Belle told me where to go in the end. We were working on a rewrite this morning,' Dominic added hastily. 'I don't want any more misunderstandings.'

'I know, Max told me. They really are married?'

'They really are. As soon as filming is

finished they're off on honeymoon. So,' Dominic paused, 'where does that leave us? Do you think you could possibly hitch your star to the most stubborn, difficult, infuriating man you have ever met?'

'With a dodgy knee?'

'I forgot that one,' Dominic admitted. 'And your answer? Do you think you could tell me, please?'

'I might give your proposal my consideration.'

'Is that all you've got to say?'

'For now, yes. Why don't you kiss me to seal the deal?'

As their lips met, Georgia knew her future might be a rocky ride but, whatever it held, it would be inextricably linked with Dominic's for ever.

THE END

Other titles in the
Linford Romance Library:

IN DESTINY'S WAKE

June Davies

Accused of stealing a necklace of pearls, Maud Pemberton flees Yorkshire to escape imprisonment. Henry Broome, her sweetheart, helps her begin a new life alone on the Lancashire coast. There, she encounters enigmatic innkeeper, Lawrence Kearsley, who conceals a family secret and when Henry unexpectedly arrives, Maud finds that he, too, harbours a dangerous secret . . . Caught within a spiral of lies and intrigue, Maud risks all to save her love from the dreadful consequences of long-buried deception.

PROMISES OF SPRING

Jean M. Long

Sophie, who's in between jobs and recovering from a broken relationship, offers to help out her Aunt Rose in Kent. Reluctantly, she finds herself being drawn into village affairs. Keir Ellison, a neighbour, is heavily involved in plans for a Craft Centre, but there is much opposition from the older residents who have different ideas for the old chapel. Sophie is attracted to Keir, but soon realises he's a man of mystery. Can she trust him?

LOVE IN PERIL

Phyllis Mallett

1792: Travelling on the long journey from London to Cornwall to meet her estranged father, Hester is plunged into peril when her coach is held up. She escapes and narrowly avoids falling victim to smugglers, due to the timely appearance of Hal Trevian. Hal takes her to her father, but, instead of finding security, other problems arise . . . although Hal is always there to support her. Will their interest in each other ever turn to love?

FAMILY HOLIDAY

Denise Robins

The summer for Clare, Guy and the children brought the holiday — like every other year. It also brought the chance meeting with Blake Randall, the young officer she'd loved years ago in a wartime hospital. And whereas Guy was the kindly but unexciting doctor she had married, Blake and Clare felt the same spark of their youth. Soon they were unashamedly head over heels in love again, but when the holiday ended, she would be separated from Blake forever . . .